Fifteen Dogs

An Apologue

ANDRÉ ALEXIS

Coach House Books, Toronto

first edition, twelfth printing

Published with the generous assistance of the Canada Council for the Arts and the Ontario Arts Council. Coach House Books also acknowledges the support of the Government of Canada through the Canada Book Fund and the Government of Ontario through the Ontario Book Publishing Tax Credit and the Ontario Book Fund.

LIBRARY AND ARCHIVES CANADA CATALOGUING IN PUBLICATION

Alexis, André, 1957-, author
    Fifteen dogs / André Alexis.

Issued in print and electronic formats.
ISBN 978-1-55245-305-6 (pbk.).

    I. Title.

PS8551.L474F53 2014   C813'.54   C2014-907934-6

Fifteen Dogs is available as an ebook: ISBN 978 1 77056 403 9

Purchase of the print version of this book entitles you to a free digital copy. To claim your ebook of this title, please email sales@chbooks.com with proof of purchase or visit chbooks.com/digital. (Coach House Books reserves the right to terminate the free digital download offer at any time.)

For Linda Watson

por qué es de día, por qué vendrá la noche …
— Pablo Neruda, '*Oda al perro*'

why is there day, why must night come …
— Pablo Neruda, '*Ode to a Dog*'

DRAMATIS CANES

AGATHA	an old Labradoodle
ATHENA	a brown teacup Poodle
ATTICUS	an imposing Neapolitan Mastiff, with cascading jowls
BELLA	a Great Dane, Athena's closest pack mate
BENJY	a resourceful and conniving Beagle
BOBBIE	an unfortunate Duck Toller
DOUGIE	a Schnauzer, friend to Benjy
FRICK	a Labrador Retriever
FRACK	a Labrador Retriever, Frick's litter mate
LYDIA	a Whippet and Weimaraner cross, tormented and nervous
MAJNOUN	a black Poodle, briefly referred to as 'Lord Jim' or simply 'Jim'
MAX	a mutt who detests poetry
PRINCE	a mutt who composes poetry, also called Russell or Elvis
RONALDINHO	a mutt who deplores the condescension of humans
ROSIE	a German Shepherd bitch, close to Atticus

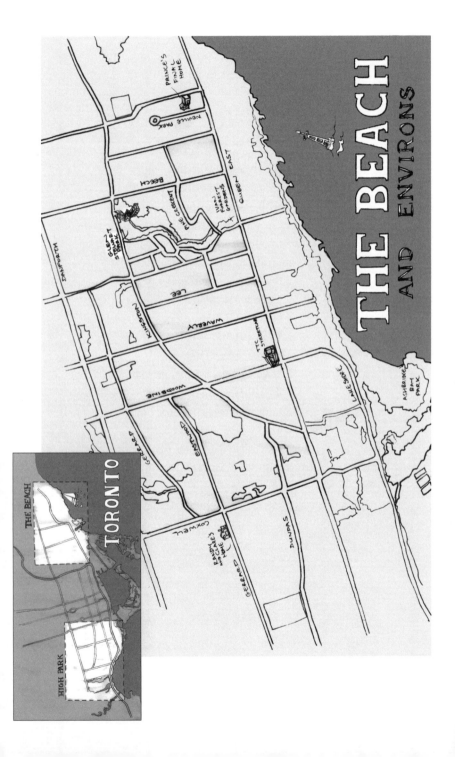

THE BEACH AND ENVIRONS

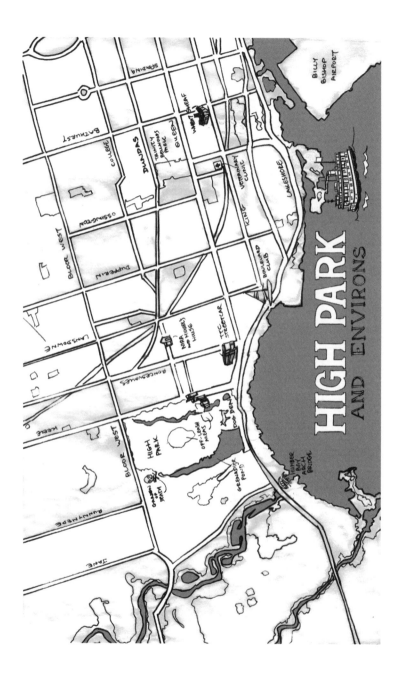

HIGH PARK AND ENVIRONS

1

A WAGER

One evening in Toronto, the gods Apollo and Hermes were at the Wheat Sheaf Tavern. Apollo had allowed his beard to grow until it reached his clavicle. Hermes, more fastidious, was clean-shaven, but his clothes were distinctly terrestrial: black jeans, a black leather jacket, a blue shirt.

They had been drinking, but it wasn't the alcohol that intoxicated them. It was the worship their presence elicited. The Wheat Sheaf felt like a temple, and the gods were gratified. In the men's washroom, Apollo allowed parts of himself to be touched by an older man in a business suit. This pleasure, more intense than any he had known or would ever know again, cost the man eight years of his life.

While at the tavern, the gods began a desultory conversation about the nature of humanity. For amusement, they spoke ancient Greek, and Apollo argued that, as creatures go, humans were neither better nor worse than any other, neither better nor worse than fleas or elephants, say. Humans, said Apollo, have no special merit, though they think themselves superior. Hermes took the opposing view, arguing that, for one thing, the human way of creating and using symbols, is more interesting than, say, the complex dancing done by bees.

— Human languages are too vague, said Apollo.

— That may be, said Hermes, but it makes humans more amusing. Just listen to these people. You'd swear they understood each other, though not one of them has any idea what their words actually mean to another. How can you resist such farce?

— I didn't say they weren't amusing, answered Apollo. But frogs and flies are amusing, too.

— If you're going to compare humans to flies, we'll get nowhere. And you know it.

In perfect though divinely accented English — that is, in an English that every patron at the tavern heard in his or her own accent — Apollo said

— Who'll pay for our drinks?

— I will, said a poor student. Please, let me.

Apollo put a hand on the young man's shoulder.

— My brother and I are grateful, he said. We've had five Sleemans each, so you'll not know hunger or want for ten years.

The student knelt to kiss Apollo's hand and, when the gods had gone, discovered hundreds of dollars in his pockets. In fact, for as long as he had the pants he was wearing that evening, he had more money in his pockets than he could spend, and it was ten years to the instant before their corduroy rotted to irrecoverable shreds.

Outside the tavern, the gods walked west along King Street.

— I wonder, said Hermes, what it would be like if animals had human intelligence.

— I wonder if they'd be as unhappy as humans, Apollo answered.

— Some humans are unhappy; others aren't. Their intelligence is a difficult gift.

— I'll wager a year's servitude, said Apollo, that animals — any animal you choose — would be even more unhappy than humans are, if they had human intelligence.

— An earth year? I'll take that bet, said Hermes, but on condition that if, at the end of its life, even one of the creatures is happy, I win.

— But that's a matter of chance, said Apollo. The best lives sometimes end badly and the worst sometimes end well.

— True, said Hermes, but you can't know what a life has been until it is over.

— Are we speaking of happy beings or happy lives? No, never mind. Either way, I accept your terms. Human intelligence is not a gift. It's an occasionally useful plague. What animals do you choose?

As it happened, the gods were not far from the veterinary clinic at Shaw. Entering the place unseen and imperceptible, they found dogs, mostly: pets left overnight by their owners for one reason or another. So, dogs it was.

— Shall I leave them their memories? asked Apollo.

— Yes, said Hermes.

With that, the god of light granted 'human intelligence' to the fifteen dogs who were in the kennel at the back of the clinic.

Somewhere around midnight, Rosie, a German shepherd, stopped as she was licking her vagina and wondered how long she would be in the place she found herself. She then wondered what had happened to the last litter she'd whelped. It suddenly seemed grossly unfair that one should go through the trouble of having pups only to lose track of them.

She got up to have a drink of water and to sniff at the hard pellets that had been left for her to eat. Nosing the food around in its shallow bowl, she was perplexed to discover that the bowl was not dark in the usual way but had, rather, a strange hue. The bowl was astonishing. It was only a kind of bubble-gum pink, but as Rosie had never seen the colour before, it looked beautiful. To her dying day, no colour ever surpassed it.

In the cell beside Rosie's, a grey Neapolitan mastiff named Atticus was dreaming of a wide field, which, to his delight, was overrun by small, furry animals, thousands of them — rats, cats, rabbits and squirrels – moving across the grass like the hem of a dress being pulled away, just out of his reach. This was Atticus's favourite dream, a recurring joy that always ended with him happily bringing a struggling creature back to his beloved master. His master would take the thing, strike it against a rock, then move his hand along Atticus's back and speak his name. Always, the dream *always* ended this way. But not this night. This night, as Atticus bit down at the neck of one of the creatures, it occurred to him that the creature must feel pain. That thought – vivid and unprecedented – woke him from sleep.

All around the kennel, dogs woke from sleep, startled by strange dreams or suddenly aware of some indefinable change in their environment. Those who had not been sleeping – it is always difficult to sleep away from home – got up and moved to the doors of their cells to see who had entered, so human did this silence feel. At first, each of them assumed that his or her newfound vision was unique. Only gradually did it become clear that all of them shared the strange world they were now living in.

A black poodle named Majnoun barked softly. He stood still, as if contemplating Rosie, who was in the cage facing his. As it happened, however, Majnoun was thinking about the lock on Rosie's cage: an elongated loop fixed to a sliding bolt. The long loop lay between two pieces of metal, effectively keeping the bolt in place and locking the cage door. It was simple, elegant and effective. And yet, to unlock the cage, all one had to do was lift the loop and push the bolt back. Standing on his hind legs and pushing a paw out of his cage, Majnoun did just that. It took him a number of attempts and it was awkward, but after a little while his cage was unlocked and he pushed the door open.

Though most of the dogs understood how Majnoun had opened his cell, not all of them were capable of doing the same. There were various reasons for this. Frick and Frack, two Labrador yearlings who had been left overnight for neutering, were too young and impatient for the doors. The smaller dogs – a chocolate teacup poodle named Athena, a schnauzer named Dougie, a beagle named Benjy – knew they were physically incapable of reaching the bolt and whined their frustration until their cells were opened for them. The older dogs, in particular a Labradoodle named Agatha, were too tired and confused to think clearly and hesitated to choose liberty, even after their doors had been opened for them.

The dogs, of course, already possessed a common language. It was language stripped to its essence, a language in which what mattered was social standing and physical need. All of them understood its crucial phrases and thoughts: 'forgive me,' 'I will bite you,' 'I am hungry.' Naturally, the imposition of primate thinking on the dogs changed how the dogs spoke to each other and to themselves. For instance: whereas previously there had been no word for 'door,' it was now understood that 'door' was a thing distinct from one's need for liberty, that 'door' existed independently of dogs. Curiously, the word for 'door' in the dogs' new language was not derived from the doors to their cells but came, rather, from the back door to the clinic itself. This back door, large and green, was opened by pushing a metal bar that almost bisected it. The sound of the metal bar, when pushed, was a thick, reverberant *thwack*. From that night on, the dogs agreed that the word for *door* should be a click (tongue on upper palate) followed by a sigh.

To say that the dogs were bewildered is to understate it. If they were 'bewildered' when the change in consciousness came over them, what were they when, all having left the clinic by the back door, they looked out on Shaw Street and suddenly understood that they were helplessly free, the door to the clinic having closed behind them, the world before them a chaos of noise and odour whose meaning now mattered to them as it had never mattered before?

Where were they? Who was to lead them?

For three of the dogs, the strange episode ended here. Agatha, who was in constant and terrible pain and had been left at the clinic to be put down, could find no point in going on with the others. She had lived a good life, had had three litters and, so, had had all the respect she needed from the bitches she sometimes met while out with her mistress. She wanted no part of a world in which her mistress did not figure. She lay down by the clinic's door and let the others know she would not leave. She did not know that this decision meant her death. It did not occur to her – it *could* not – that her mistress had left her to face death on her own. The worst of it was, the following morning, when those working at the clinic discovered her – along with the mutts, Ronaldinho and Lydia – they were not kind. They took their frustration out on Agatha, hurting her as she was brought to the silver table where she was to be put down. One of the workers slapped her as she raised her head in an effort to bite him. She knew as soon as she saw the table that the end had come, and her final moments were spent in a useless effort to communicate her desire to see her mistress. In her confusion, Agatha hoarsely barked the word for 'hunger' over and over until her spirit was released from her body.

Though Ronaldinho and Lydia lived longer than Agatha, their ends were almost as unhappy. Both had been left at the clinic for minor ailments. Both were sent home to grateful owners. And in both cases their new ways of thinking poisoned what had been (or what they remembered as being) idyllic and relatively long lives. Ronaldinho lived with a family that loved him, but at his return from the clinic he began to notice how condescending they were. Despite the palpable evidence that Ronaldinho had changed, the family treated him as no more than a plaything. He learned their language. He would sit, stand, play dead, roll over or beg before the commands were entirely spoken. He learned to turn off the stove when the kettle's whistle sounded. And once, when it was asserted in his presence that dogs could not count to twenty, he stared at the person who'd said so and barked – ironically, bitterly – twenty times. No one noticed or cared. Worse: perhaps because they suspected Ronaldinho was 'not his old self,' the family shunned him somewhat, perfunctorily petting his back or head as if in memory of the dog he had once been. He died bitter and disillusioned.

Lydia fared worse. A cross between a whippet (her mother) and a Weimaraner, she had always been something of a nervous creature.

The advent of human intelligence made her more nervous still. She, too, learned the language of her masters, scrupulously doing or anticipating whatever was wanted of her. She did not mind their condescension. She minded that they were inattentive and neglectful, because along with 'primate mind' there came an acute awareness of time. The passage of time, each moment like a scabies mite crawling under her skin, was an unbearable scourge. The scourge was assuaged only by the presence of her masters, by their company. As her masters, a professional couple who smelled of lilacs and citrus, were often away for eight hours at a stretch, however, Lydia's suffering was terrible. She would bark, howl and plead for hours on end. Finally, when her mind could no longer bear the repeated agony, it chanced on a typically human haven from suffering: catatonia. One day, her masters discovered her in the living room, her legs rigid, her eyes unclosed. They took her to the clinic on Shaw, and when the vet told them there was nothing he could do, they had her put down. They had not been considerate masters but they were sentimental. They buried Lydia in their back garden, planting – in her honour – a carpet of yellow flowers (*Genista lydia*) on the mound that marked her resting place.

The twelve who set out from Shaw were driven as much by confusion as anything else. The world seemed new and marvellous and yet it was familiar and banal. Nothing should have surprised them, yet everything did. The pack moved warily, going south on Strachan: over the bridge, down to the lake.

They were, it has to be said, almost instinctively drawn to the lakeshore. Its confluence of reeks was as bewitching to the dogs as the smell of an early-morning bakery is to humans. There was, first, the lake itself: sour, vegetal, fishy. Then there was the smell of geese, ducks and other birds. More enticing still, there was the smell of bird shit, which was like a kind of hard salad sautéed in goose fat. Finally, there were more evanescent whiffs: cooked pork, tomatoes, grease from cow's meat, corn, bread, sweetness and milk. None of them could resist it, though there was little shelter by the lake, few places to hide if masters came for them.

None could resist the lake, but it occurred to Majnoun that they should. It occurred to him that the city was the worst place for them to be, filled as it was with beings that feared dogs who would not do their bidding. What they needed, thought Majnoun, was a place where they would be safe until they decided on a course that was good for all of them. It also occurred to him that Atticus, who was at the head of the pack, was not necessarily the one to lead. It wasn't that he himself wanted to lead. Though he was swept up in the present adventure and fairly happy to be with the others, Majnoun was more comfortable around humans. He did not trust other dogs. This made the thought of leadership unpleasant to him. The true things – food, shelter, water – would have to be dealt with by all, but who would lead, and whom would he choose to follow?

It was dark, though the moon fell out of its pocket of clouds from time to time. Four in the morning, the world full of shadows. The gates to the Canadian National Exhibition loomed as if they might totter and crush anything beneath them. There were not many cars, but Majnoun waited for the green light at the bottom of the street. Half of the pack – Rosie, Athena, Benjy, an Albertan mutt named Prince and a Duck Toller called Bobbie – waited with him. The other half – Frick, Frack, Dougie, Bella the Great Dane, and a mutt named Max – blithely crossed the boulevard with Atticus.

Once they had all crossed, the dark and shushing lake lay before them, while along the promenade lay various types of dung, various bits of food, and other things to be sniffed out. Atticus, a crumpled-face dog whose instinct was to hunt, could also feel the presence of small animals, rats and mice most likely, and he wanted to go after them. He exhorted the others to hunt with him.

– Why? asked Majnoun.

The question – asked with an innovation of the dogs' common language – was stunning. Atticus had never considered that it might be right to hold himself back from rats, birds or food. He considered the 'why?,' distractedly licking his snout as he did. Finally, innovating in language himself, he said

— Why not?

Frick and Frack, delighted, immediately agreed.

— Why not? they asked. Why not?

— Where will we hide if a master comes? answered Majnoun.

A more subtle question no dog could have asked. The assumptions behind it felt both right and yet strangely wrong. Majnoun, though he respected his own master, assumed the dogs would all want to hide from their masters. Freedom, thought Majnoun, came before respect. But the word *master* evoked in all of them feelings that did and did not call for hiding. For some, the idea of a master was comforting. Prince, who since coming to the city had been separated from Kim, his master, would have done anything to find him. Athena, all three and a half pounds of her, was used to being carried wherever she went. She was exhausted already, having kept up with the pack for such a long stretch. Faced with all the walking they would have to do, faced with the uncertainty that now seemed to be their lot, she thought she would happily submit to one who fed her and carried her about. However, as most of the other, bigger dogs seemed to dislike the idea of submission, she pretended to dislike it as well.

Even Majnoun's position was not without subtlety or ambivalence. He had always been proud of his ability to do what his master asked. He had earned the biscuits and treats that had come to him, but he had resented the ritual, too. He had sometimes had to suppress himself to keep from running away. In fact, he would have fled his master, had he been able to take the treats with him — not just the treats, mind you, but the whole *feeling* of treats, the being patted, the being spoken to in the way his master spoke when pleased. Of course, now that he was free, there was no use thinking about treats at all.

Frick and Frack, both too immature to have fully understood or experienced the pleasures of servitude, were the only ones entirely in agreement with Majnoun's suggestion that they would need a hiding place at the appearance of a master.

Atticus, whose feelings were as nuanced as Majnoun's, never-theless said

— Why hide? Don't we have teeth?

He bared his teeth and all understood the terrible suggestion.

— I couldn't bite my mistress, said Athena. She would not be pleased.

— I do not know what to say, said Atticus.

— The small bitch is not wrong, said Majnoun. If we were to bite masters, other masters would notice us and resent our freedom. I have seen many free dogs beaten. We should not bite unless we are attacked. And we should find shelter.

— All this talking, said Atticus. It is not like dogs to talk so much. We'll find food. Then we'll look for shelter.

They went hunting. That is, some went in search of what they knew as food and others went after the animals they atavistically associated with sustenance. They were tremendously successful. Their instincts led them infallibly to the small animals — four rats, five squirrels — that they killed with ingenious efficiency, corralling or ambushing the poor creatures. After two hours, as the morning sun lit the land and turned the lake bluish green, there were rats, squirrels, hot dog buns, bits of hamburger, handfuls of French fries, half-eaten apples, and sugary confections so covered in dirt it was difficult to say what they had been. The only real disappointment was that they had not managed to catch any geese. Also: most of the dogs resisted the small animals and went for the scraps of human food. They left the headless, half-chewed remains of rats and squirrels in a neat row on the hill beside the Boulevard Club.

In the days that followed, there were a number of signs — both subtle and obvious — that their newfound thoughtfulness had led to collective change. To begin with, a new language flowered within them, changing the way they communicated. This change was espe-cially evident in Prince. He was constantly finding words within himself, words he shared with the others. It was Prince, for instance, who came up with the word for 'human' (roughly: *grrr-ahhi*, the sound of a growl followed a sound typical of humans). This was a significant accomplishment, as the dogs could now speak of the primates without speaking of mastery. It was also Prince who devised what might be called the dogs' first witticism: the word for 'bone' in the new language (roughly: *rrr-eye*) and the word for 'stone' (roughly: *rrr-eeye*) were very close. When Prince was asked one evening what he was eating, he replied 'stone' while indicating a bone. A number of the dogs found this – the first conspicuous pun in the language – both diverting and right, suggesting as it did that the bones in question were difficult to chew.

Then, too, they became sharper hunters and more discriminating scavengers as they became intimate with their territory: Parkdale and High Park, from Bloor to the lake, from Windemere to Strachan. All quickly learned the places where they could congregate without attracting undue human – or canine – attention. Moreover: spurred by Prince's observations of sunlight and shadow, they learned to segment the day into useful units. That is, collectively, they discovered a use for time, which discovery was salve for their awareness of its passing. (Day, from the first appearance of sun to the first moment of its descent, was broken into eight unequal units, each of which was given a name. Night, from the first quieting of the world to the first noisy birds, was broken into eleven. In this way, the dogs' day was made up of nineteen units, rather than twenty-four.)

It was, in part, this new relationship to time and place that influenced the creation of their den. Atticus, practical and persuasive (though he mistrusted the new language from the beginning), suggested they take over a coppice in High Park, a clearing beneath a cluster of evergreens, to which they brought tennis balls, running shoes, human clothing, blankets, squeaky toys ... anything they could find or steal to make the place more hospitable. They did not intend to stay in the coppice forever. It was, Atticus said, makeshift and temporary, a place to meet at the start of night, but it soon began to feel as if it were theirs. It smelled of pine gum, dog and urine.

Perhaps the most striking sign that 'primate thinking' could be useful, however, was in the relationship between Bella and Athena. The two were, of course, at opposite ends of the scale where weight and height were concerned. They were the same age – that is, three – but Athena was all of three or four pounds and her legs were short. She could not keep up with the others when the pack moved. Bella was three or four feet tall and weighed somewhere around two hundred pounds. She did not often run. Rather, though she wasn't the most thoughtful of dogs, she moved with something like deliberation, majestically. Seeing Athena could not keep up with them and remembering how a four-year-old girl had ridden on her back, Bella offered to let Athena ride.

This was no problem for Bella. She knelt, her front legs tucked under her, and waited for Athena to climb up. This Athena did, but in the early going she would almost immediately fall off again and it hurt to fall from Bella's back. She learned quickly, though. By the third day, using her claws to steady herself and biting into Bella's neck to keep in place, Athena was so well balanced it would have been difficult to dislodge her. This made for an especially curious sight when, after a few days, Bella – with her loping and rhythmically arrhythmic gait – felt confident enough to run if she wanted, her withers dipping and rising while Athena, like a furry passenger on a ship's fo'c'sle, joyfully held on.

Exhilarating as this was for the bitches – and the two were soon as close as litter mates – the arrangement caused trouble for the pack. Athena and Bella brought unwanted attention. One day, as the dogs were scavenging for food along the lakeshore, a group of young human males noticed the way Athena rode on Bella's back. Amused and immediately scornful, they began to chase after the dogs. Strange in the way that humans are strange, the high spirits of the young males were, to Bella and Athena, indistinguishable from aggression or dislike. The boys took up rocks and began to throw them at the dogs. Bella was not fast and she could not run for long distances at a stretch. After a while, she slowed and one of the rocks hit Athena, who yelped in pain and fell from Bella's back. Athena's misfortune and pain provoked even greater amusement in the humans. They gathered more rocks, intent now on causing the dogs as much distress as they could.

Though Bella was by nature even-tempered and difficult to rile, as the young males approached she was at once protective and ready to kill. Using the only guile that occurred to her, counting on taking out the biggest of her attackers first, she went at them snarling and single-minded. And she was on the leader before he or any of the others could react or run away. Launching her two hundred pounds at him, she went instinctively for his throat and, had he not raised his arm at the last moment, she would have bitten through the flesh of his neck. Instead, she bit his right hand straight down to the bone. Blood spurted as he cried out beneath her. The others, though armed with stones, were petrified. They stood still, listening to their friend cry for help. Their fear worked entirely to Bella's advantage. In an instant, she was off the first human, done with him, running directly at the next one closest to her. He ran off at once, screeching in distress, leaving his friends to their fate.

Atticus and Majnoun, who had been scavenging nearby and had come at the sounds of an affray, snarled at the humans and ran after them, chasing them farther off, ensuring they did not turn back, though, in fact, turning back was the furthest thing from any of their minds. The rout, in other words, was thorough and swift. The six or seven boys, none of them older than fourteen, were traumatized and humiliated. But when the dogs saw that Athena was not badly hurt – she had bled and there was a clump of wet fur above her left eye – Majnoun said

– This is not good. Humans don't like it when you bite them. We will have to change territory.

– I agree it is not good, said Atticus, but why should we leave? They will be looking for these two. The bitches will have to keep out of sight. The big one is the one who did damage. They will come for her, but they will not come for us.

– I do not agree and I do not disagree, said Majnoun.

But the dogs took precautions. Bella and Athena scavenged in High Park and stayed close to the coppice. They kept away from the lakeshore and Athena did not travel on Bella's back until evening, when shadow obscured them. During the day, the others went about in small groups, no more than two or three together, drawing as little attention as possible.

These precautions were taken for the sake of humans. It wasn't that humans were inevitably dangerous, but they were unpredictable. While one might kneel to pat your back or scratch your beard, another who looked exactly like the first would kick you, throw stones, or even do you to death. It was, in general, best to avoid them. Contrary to expectations, however, in the first weeks after their change, the worst confrontations were not with humans but with other dogs. No matter how polite the pack were or how non-committal, some would attack them at once, without so much as a snarl or a baring of teeth.

– They think we're weak, said Atticus.

But it wasn't as simple as that. The dogs who attacked were aggressive, but they also seemed afraid. They weren't frightened of the bigger dogs alone, of Bella or Atticus, Frick or Frack. They were also intimidated by Dougie, Benjy, Bobbie and Athena, none of whom should have been threatening to any reasonably sized creature. The dogs who did not immediately attack them were, at times, immediately submissive, and this was almost as strange. It was, to the smaller dogs, as if they were being mistaken for fierce and towering versions of themselves.

The twelve dogs reacted differently to their altered status. Atticus found the situation intolerable. It was traumatic to know oneself to be a simple dog but to live in a world where other dogs treated you as something other. For Atticus, all the old pleasures – sniffing at an anus, burying one's nose where a friend's genitals were, mounting those with lower status – could no longer be had without crippling self-consciousness. In this, he, Majnoun, Prince and Rosie were alike.

The four of them were inclined to a thoughtfulness that all save Prince – and to an extent, Majnoun – would have abandoned in order to lose themselves once more in the community of dogs. Prince was the only one who entirely embraced the change in consciousness. It was as if he'd discovered a new way of seeing, an angle that made all that he had known strange and wonderful.

At the other end of the spectrum were Frick, Frack and the mutt, Max. They, too, were troubled by self-consciousness, but they learned to suppress thinking. They used their newfound thoughtfulness, certainly, but they did so while remaining faithful to the old way of being dogs. When challenged by unknown dogs, they defended themselves with lascivious efficiency, ganging up on their attackers, treating them the way they would sheep: biting through their tendons, leaving them to bleed and suffer. When they encountered submissive dogs, their pleasure was just as intense. The three would fuck anything that let them. In a way, then, their new (or different) intelligence was at the service of what they understood to be their essence: the canine. They were worthy of the fear 'normal' dogs showed them.

In fact, the dogs that caused Frick, Frack and Max the most trouble were the others in their own pack. Yes, the other nine shared their intelligence and swiftly evolving language. And, yes, the others were the only creatures who understood them. But 'understanding,' reeking as it did of thought, was the last thing they wanted. 'Understanding' was a reminder that, despite their efforts to live as dogs, they were no longer normal. What they wanted from the others was submission or leadership and, at first, they got neither.

Of the other dogs, Prince was, naturally, the one who annoyed Frick, Frack and Max most. Prince was a mutt of some sort, his fur russet with a white patch on his chest. He was big but his disposition nullified any physical threat. He was never less than accommodating. He could be dominated. The irritant was that Prince had strange ideas. It was he who had divided the day into portions. It was he who asked endless questions about trivial things: about humans, about the sea, about trees, about his favourite smells (bird flesh, grass, hot dogs), about the yellow disk above them in whose light one could be warm. The three had, of course, loathed Prince's pun on 'stone' and 'bone.' Nor would Prince stop. Encouraged by the others, his play with language was a constant affront to clarity.

It seemed to Frick and Frack as if Prince were intent on destroying their spirit.

But Prince's witticisms were not the worst of it. Previously, they, like all dogs, had made do with a simple vocabulary of fundamental sounds: bark, howl or snarl. These sounds were acceptable, as were useful innovations, like the word for 'water' or the one for 'human.' At Prince's instigation, however, the pack now had words for countless things. (Did any dog really need a word for 'dust'?) Then, one night, Prince sat up and spoke a strange group of words:

> The grass is wet on the hill.
> The sky has no end.
> For the dog who waits for his mistress,
> Madge, noon comes again.

Hearing this grouping of growls, barks, yips and sighs, Frack and Frick had jumped up, ready to bite the face off the weary dog's mistress. They assumed a master was among them, ready to inflict pain. But Prince's words had not been meant as warning. Rather, he had been playing. He had been pretending. He had been speaking for speaking's sake. Could there be a more despicable use for words? Max got up, snarling, ready to bite.

He had not counted on the pleasure some of the others had taken in Prince's words, however. Athena thanked Prince for his evocation of wet hills and endless skies. Bella did the same. Far from feeling that Prince had abused their tongue, a number of the dogs felt that – as with his play with words – he'd brought something unexpected and wonderful to it.

– I was moved, said Majnoun. Please, do it again.

Prince performed another set of howls, barks, yips and clicks.

Beyond the hills, a master is
who knows our secret names.
With bell and bones, he'll call us home,
winter, fall or spring.

Most of the dogs sat in silence, no doubt trying to understand what Prince was on about. But it was too much for Max. It wasn't just that Prince was twisting their clear, noble language, it was that Prince had gone beyond the canine. No true dog could have uttered such tripe. Prince was not worthy of being one of them. In defence of their true nature, someone had to do something. Max could sense that Frack and Frick felt as he did, but he wanted to be the first to bite Prince into submission or force him into exile. He charged at Prince without so much as a growl. Prince was at his mercy. He was about to bite the mutt's throat when, as quietly and viciously as Max had attacked, Majnoun came to Prince's defence. Before Frick or Frack could intervene, Majnoun had Max down, his teeth securely in Max's throat. Max peed in submission and lay still.

– Don't kill him, said Frack.

Majnoun growled in warning, bit down harder, drawing blood.

– The dog is right, said Atticus. It is not good to kill one of our own.

Majnoun felt – with every fibre in him – that killing Max was the right thing. It was as if he knew the time would come when he'd be obliged to kill him. So why not now? But he listened to Atticus and released Max, who slunk quickly away, his tail between his legs.

– There was no need for violence, said Atticus. The dog was only trying to show his feelings about the words we heard.

– His feelings were not hidden, said Majnoun.

– You have shown him his place, said Atticus. You did right.

Aside from Frack and Frick – who were deliberately unthoughtful – most of the dogs were bemused by what had passed between Max and Majnoun. In the old days, one would have said they had witnessed a struggle for dominance, a struggle that Majnoun had clearly won and, so, increased his status. But, here, there was the matter of Prince. Prince had offended Max. His *words* had offended. So, had Max and Majnoun fought over words or status? Could dogs fight to the death over words? It was strange to think so.

As Bella and Athena lay beside each other on the verge of sleep, Athena said

– These males fight for any reason.

– It has nothing to do with us, said Bella.

That was the end of the matter, as far as they were concerned, and the two were soon asleep, Athena growling quietly at a squirrel that, in her dream, was much smaller than she and deliberately annoying besides.

Two evenings after the fracas, Atticus spoke to Majnoun.

Autumn had come. The leaves were changing colour. Night itself seemed darker, for being more cool. The pack had settled into a routine: scavenging, avoiding humans, hunting rats and squirrels. The coppice provided shelter from rainfall and storms. So, although they had meant it to be a temporary dwelling, a place from which they could consider what had happened to them, the coppice had become a home, and it was increasingly difficult to imagine leaving it.

Majnoun had been expecting some sort of approach from Frick, Frack, Max or Atticus. He had expected one of them to bring up the matter of leadership. The pack had done without a leader for some time, an unnatural situation. And although he himself did not want to lead, it would have been an insult for the others to foist Atticus – the likeliest candidate – on the pack without seeking his (that is, Majnoun's) opinion first. In the old days, they would have fought about it, no doubt. But after the change that had come over them, a physical contest no longer seemed, to Majnoun at least, the best way to resolve a matter as complicated as leadership.

(How odd the change was! One day, while listening to humans address their pet, Majnoun experienced a curious thing. It was as if the sun had, in an instant, burned off a thick morning fog. He understood what the humans were saying! It wasn't just some of their words he understood – words he'd heard a thousand times himself. He believed he understood the thought behind them. As far as Majnoun knew, no dog had ever understood a human as he had at that moment. He wasn't sure if he were cursed or blessed, but this new thing – this *understanding* – surely demanded a change in behaviour, something to help them deal with the unabated strangeness of the new world.)

Majnoun and Atticus walked out of the coppice together and into the park. The sky was filled with stars. The lights of the Queensway were off to the south. All was quiet, save for the endless noise of the crickets, it not being cold enough to silence them.

– What are we to do? asked Atticus.

The question was a surprise.

– About what? answered Majnoun.

– I have asked the wrong question, said Atticus. I mean, how are we to live, now that we are strangers to our own kind?

– They are right to be afraid of us, said Majnoun. We no longer think like they do.

– But we feel like they feel, don't we? I remember what I was before that night. I am not so different.

– I did not know you before, said Majnoun, but I know you now and now you are different.

– Some of us, said Atticus, believe the best way is to ignore the new thinking and stop using the new words.

– How can you silence the words inside?

– No one can silence the words inside, but you can ignore them. We can go back to the old way of being. This new thinking leads away from the pack, but a dog is no dog if he does not belong.

– I do not agree, said Majnoun. We have this new way. It has been given to us. Why should we not use it? Maybe there is a reason for our difference.

– I remember, said Atticus, how it was to run with our kind. But you, you want to think and keep thinking and then think again. What is the good of so much thinking? I am like you. I can take

31

pleasure in it, but it brings us no true advantage. It keeps us from being dogs and it keeps us from what is right.

— We know things other dogs do not. Can we not teach them?

— No, said Atticus. Now it is for them to teach us. We must learn to be dogs again.

— Dog, why do you want my thoughts on these things? Do you wish to lead?

— Would you challenge me?

— No, said Majnoun.

The dogs sat together awhile, listening to the sounds of night. In the park, the world was teeming with unseen life. Above them was a vastness as new and haunting as it was ancient. Neither of them had ever paid much attention to stars and the night sky. Now they could not help wondering about it.

— I wonder if the dog who speaks strangely is right, said Atticus. Does the sky really have no end?

— The dog thinks beautifully, said Majnoun, but he knows no more than we do.

— Do you think we will ever know?

Majnoun struggled with the question and struggled with the thoughts within him. All sometimes seemed so hopelessly muddled. He wondered if Atticus wasn't right, in the end. Perhaps it was best to be a dog as dogs had always been: not separated from others by thinking but part of the collective. Perhaps anything else was futile or, worse, an illusion to take you away from the good. But although their new way of thinking was bothersome — a torment at times — it was now an aspect of them. Why should they turn their backs on themselves?

— Someday, said Majnoun, we may know where the sky ends.

— Yes, said Atticus, someday or someday not.

Majnoun's instincts were sound. He'd anticipated a tête-à-tête about leadership and, although Atticus had kept the discussion vague, it *had* been about power. Majnoun, however, had not caught all the nuances. Atticus was not interested in whether or not Majnoun would challenge him for leadership. Atticus was bigger than Majnoun and, besides, he had Frick, Frack, Max and Rosie on his side. What Atticus had really wanted to discover was whether Majnoun belonged with the pack, given the direction that he, Atticus, had chosen for it. Majnoun, unawares, had given Atticus all the information he needed.

The following day, when they were meant to be out scavenging, Frack, Frick, Max and Atticus met by the lake on the far side of the Humber Bay Arch Bridge, away from the others, away from dogs without leashes.

— I have spoken with all the others, said Atticus. To live as we were meant to live, there must be change. Some may stay. Some must not.

— What about the black dog? asked Frack.

— He is not one of us, answered Atticus. He will have to be exiled.

— It would be better to kill him, said Max.

— You only think so because he mounted you, said Frick.

— No, said Atticus, the dog is right. The black one will not be easy to send away. Some of the others are already faithful to him. I do not wish to kill him, but it would be difficult if he stayed.

— What about the bitch with the high vagina? asked Max.

— She favours the black dog and she is too strong, said Atticus. We will have to lose her.

— Let her take the tiny bitch with her, said Max.

— What about rules? asked Frack.

— There will be two, answered Atticus. No language but proper dog language, and no ways but dog ways. We will live like we were meant to.

— Without masters? asked Frick.

— We will have no masters, said Atticus. Dogs without masters are the only true dogs. There are three who will have to go: the big bitch, the black dog and the one who uses words in strange ways. Once they have gone, we can live as we are meant to.

— Are you going to challenge the black dog? asked Max.

– No, said Atticus. We must get rid of all three at once. We will be quick and do what has to be done, before the rest of the dogs can choose sides or make matters difficult.

– When? asked Frick.

– Tonight, said Atticus.

And although it was not doglike of them, they worked their strategy out to the least detail, the least detail being what they would do if their efforts failed.

Prince had spoken another poem

> The light that moves is not the light.
> The light that stays is not the light.
> The true light rose countless sleeps ago.
> It rose, even in the mouth of birds.

and Max had wanted to kill him on the spot.

After the dogs had reflected on what they'd heard, most had gone to their beddings in the den and had fallen straight to sleep, as if lulled by Prince's words. Not Atticus, however. Atticus had invited Majnoun out into the park for another conversation. Then, when the den was quiet save for the small sounds of breathing, Frick and Frack rose from their places. Frick noiselessly padded to where Bella and Athena slept, took up Athena's compact body in his jaws, bit down hard, and made off with her. Despite Athena's strangled shriek, none of the other dogs woke.

After a time, Frack woke Bella, nudging her head with his snout.

– They have taken the small bitch, he said.

Bella rose slowly from sleep, but when she saw Athena was gone she was immediately alert and understood Frack's words.

– Where have they taken her? she asked.

– I do not know. My brother has gone after them. I will take you where they went.

Where he took her – where they ran – was to a street beside the park: Bloor. The street was on a hill and, though it was night, it was rhythmically busy. That is, groups of cars came fast down the hill and then nothing and then fast cars again. Toward the middle of the incline, on the sidewalk, Frick stood in the light of a street lamp. He was looking at something on the other side of the road.

As Bella and Frack approached, he said

– There she is. Can you see her? She is under the light.

Bella could not see clearly, but there did appear to be something beneath the street lamp on the other side of the road. It was an intimidating road, but, where Athena was concerned, Bella was not cautious. She would have done anything for this, the one being on earth to whom she was devoted. In fact, she would have run across the street at once, had Frack not said

– Wait! My brother will go to the top of the hill and bark when the light has changed and it is safe to cross.

Bella waited anxiously, jumping up and down, trying desperately to see Athena on the other side of the road.

– Go now, said Frack, it is safe.

But, of course, it was not safe. Frick's timing was impeccable. Bella was not a quarter of the way across the road before she was struck and killed by a taxi.

In a word, the murders of Bella and Athena were flawlessly done.

Being certain that Bella was dead, her body unmoving as the humans in the street raised their voices, Frick and Frack returned to the den where, it had been agreed, they and Max would finish Prince off before joining Atticus in killing Majnoun.

There should not have been any complications. Max was to have kept watch on Prince. And this he had done, though he could barely keep himself from biting the mangy mutt that had caused his humiliation. Max had (little by little and quietly) moved close to Prince, lying down near enough to hear Prince's occasional snorts and whimpers. It was not possible that Prince should have gotten away from them. And yet, when Frack and Frick slunk quietly back to the den and, joined by Max, readied themselves to finish Prince off as quickly as possible, they discovered that what they'd taken to be Prince's body was no more than a pile of human clothes. Max was beside himself with outrage. It was not possible for Prince to have escaped! He had listened for every breath, happy to know they would be among the dog's last! The three made the rounds of the den, going to where each dog lay, sniffing for Prince's smell, but Prince was nowhere to be found.

And yet, Prince was there among them.

The deaths of Bella and Athena, though straightforward as murders go, were problematic for the gods. Hermes and Apollo looked down on Athena's lifeless body (Frick had broken her neck as easily as if it had been a rat's) and on Bella's body where it had landed in the middle of the street.

— They died happy, said Hermes. I win.

— You do not win, said his brother. The small one was terrified and the large one was distressed for her friend. They died *un*happy.

— You're not being fair, said Hermes. I grant you their final moments weren't pleasant. But before they were killed, neither had known such friendship as they experienced together. They were happy despite the intelligence they were given.

— I agree with you, Apollo said, but what can I do? *You* were the one who insisted the crucial moment was death. We agreed that if even one of these creatures *dies* happy, you win. At the moment of their deaths, these two were not happy. So, you haven't won a thing. But, look, Hermes, I don't want to hear about how I cheated you and I don't want you going to Father. So, I've got a proposition for you: because your bet's not as strong as mine, I'll let you intervene in the lives of these creatures. Once. Only once. You can do whatever you like. But if you intervene, the bet's doubled. It's *two* human years of servitude to the loser.

— And you won't intervene yourself?

— Why should I intervene? asked Apollo. These creatures are more miserable than I could possibly make them. They're not going to cheer up when they die. But if it makes you feel better, I give you my word: I will not intervene directly.

– Then I accept, said Hermes.

And so, while Frick and Frack were returning from dealing with Bella and Athena, Prince had a very strange dream. It began pleasantly enough. He dreamed he was in his first master's house in Ralston, Alberta, a house in which his own scent dominated, a house over which his toys were spread in a secret pattern, a house of which he knew every cranny. He was on his way to the kitchen, drawn by the sound of mice scurrying over the wooden floor, when a dog he did not know entered his dream. The strange dog was jet black, save for a patch of vivid blue on its chest.

– You are in danger, the dog said.

The dog spoke Prince's language flawlessly, with no accent.

– How beautifully you speak, said Prince. Who are you?

– You would find my name difficult to say, said the dog, but I am Hermes and I am not of your species. I am a master of masters and I do not wish you to die here.

– Where? asked Prince.

And all of a sudden he was far from the home of his childhood. He was in High Park looking down on himself as he slept in the den with the others. He saw, because Hermes pointed it out, that Max was lying near him. He saw Frick and Frack return to the den. He noticed, because Hermes wished him to, the place where Bella and Athena had slept.

– Where is the tall female? he asked.

– They have killed her, said Hermes. They will kill you, too, if you stay.

– What have I done? asked Prince. I have not challenged anyone.

– They dislike how you speak, said Hermes. If you wish to live, your only choice is exile.

– But what am I without those who understand me?

– Would you choose words over life? asked Hermes. Consider that, if you die, your way of speaking dies with you. You must wake

37

up, now, Prince. While I am here, no one can see or hear you, but you haven't much time. Come.

There then followed the strangest interlude in Prince's life. He did not know if he were awake or dreaming, but the strange dog had spoken his secret name, the name his first master used: Prince. Rising up from the den in his dreams, he was yet with Hermes watching himself rise. He saw Frack, Frick and Max as they went about looking for him. They passed in front of him, beside him, almost *through* him. He could barely resist barking to let them know he was there, as if it were all a game. But he did not bark. He followed Hermes out of the den and into High Park proper. There, he was suddenly, fully awake and Hermes was gone.

It occurred to Prince that he was still dreaming. He thought to look in on himself, just to see if he were still asleep in the coppice, his favourite chewing shoe beside him. But as he walked back toward the den, Max, Frick and Frack ran out. Prince immediately crouched down, his ears back, his tail tucked hard behind him. The dogs did not see him. They ran off, but they radiated menace as they went. Prince had no doubt that, dream or not, Hermes had told the truth. The three were murderous. When he was certain they would not see him, he fled, his exile beginning in panic, fear and darkness.

The three who ran out of the coppice ran out to find Atticus. They had agreed that they should all attack Majnoun together. Frustrated by Prince's mysterious disappearance, Max, Frick and Frack now wanted nothing more than to bite the black dog to death. They ran toward the pond, where Atticus said they would find him, as if running to mount a bitch in heat.

For Atticus, the time spent with Majnoun was unpleasant. It was unpleasant because he understood Majnoun and was sorry the dog had to go. In other circumstances, he might have welcomed Majnoun to the pack, but things were as they were. Atticus spent much of the time surreptitiously justifying what he knew was to come: a pack needed unity, and unity meant that all understood the world in the same way or, if not the world, the rules, at least. Majnoun was one who embraced the new way of thinking, the new language. The dog did not belong.

— Black dog, said Atticus, can there be a feeling greater than belonging?

— No, said Majnoun.

— And yet, said Atticus, I am sometimes afraid that I will not know the feeling again, that I will never again know what it is to be a dog among dogs. This thinking of yours, black dog, it is an endless, dead field. Since the change, I have been alone with thoughts I do not want.

— I understand, said Majnoun. It is the same for me. But we must bear it, because we cannot escape the things within.

— I do not agree, said Atticus. To be with others is to be free from yourself. There is no other path. We must go back to the old ways.

— If we can find them, said Majnoun.

It was at this point that Frack, Frick and Max came upon them. Max said

— The tall bitch is dead.

— What has happened? asked Majnoun.

— She was attacked by our kind, a pack of them. They are near our den now.

— How many? asked Majnoun.

— Many, said Max, but they are not as big as we are.

— We must defend our home, said Atticus.

Frick and Frack ran before Majnoun, Max and Atticus on either side of him. Not far from the coppice, the brothers turned around and attacked Majnoun without warning. Max and Atticus joined in at once. The dogs were quick and merciless, and although Majnoun tried to run for shelter they had him. The four bit at Majnoun, sinking teeth into his flanks, his neck, the tendons of his legs, his stomach and genitals. Had it been daylight, the conspirators might have been gratified by the sight of Majnoun's blood. They might have been even more aroused, so intoxicating was the taste of blood and the adrenaline of murder.

If it had been day and if they had been a little less excited, they might have made certain Majnoun was dead. As it was, they went at him until he no longer resisted, until his body's spasms stopped. Then they left him for dead, returning to the coppice to begin a new life that was to be, in effect, an obsession with the old one.

2

MAJNOUN AND BENJY

When Majnoun awakened, he was in a house that smelled of peanut butter and fried liver. He lay in a wicker basket lined with a thick, orange blanket that smelled of something sweet, soapy and human. He tried to move but found he could not. It was too painful and, as well, moving was awkward. His abdomen was shaved and he was bound with white bandages that smelled of oil and pine and something indefinable. His face itched but there was a plastic cone around his head: the narrow end of the cone was cut so that the aperture fit around his neck, the wide end projecting out like a megaphone. Even if he'd wanted to scratch his face, he could not have done so. All four of his legs were shaven and bandaged. He raised his head, the better to see where he was, but he was nowhere: a whitish room with windows that looked out on a sky that was blue and bright.

During his attack – which he suddenly recalled with a vividness that was painful – he had assumed that the darkness he was falling into would be endless. He had given some thought to death in the time he'd been free and he had assumed that his death had come. This whitish room seemed to be proof he was still alive and, unexpectedly, he was disappointed. What was the point of living on after what he'd been through?

Wishing to know where he was, Majnoun raised his head higher. He tried to call out, but his voice was low and faint and it was painful to bark. Still, he barked as carefully as he could.

Behind him there came the thud of steps.

— He's awake, a voice spoke.

And the face of a human male eclipsed the room.

— How you feeling? the man asked.

The face of a human female jostled the man's face out of Majnoun's field of vision.

— You're so lucky! Aren't you lucky! Who's the lucky boy, eh? Who's the lucky boy?

— I don't think he'll be able to get up for quite a while, said the man. I wonder if he's hungry.

Hungry was a word Majnoun knew well. Using his own language, he clicked, whined and weakly barked out the words that meant he was indeed hungry.

— I know you're in pain, boy. Try not to get excited, the woman said.

Then, to the man

— I think he's too weak to eat.

— You might be right, said the man, but let's see.

The man left the room and returned with a plate of white rice and chopped chicken livers. He put the plate down in front of Majnoun (it smelled divine!), unclasped the plastic cone, and watched as Majnoun gingerly moved closer to the plate and – without sitting up – took in a mouthful of food with a sidewise swipe of his tongue.

— I guess I was wrong, said the woman. He *is* hungry.

— Why don't you name him?

— You think we should keep him?

– Why not? Once he gets better he can keep you company during the day.

– Okay. Why don't we call him Lord Jim?

– You want to name him after the world's most boring book?

– If I wanted to do that, I'd call him Golden Bowl.

Listening to the noise the humans made, Majnoun was reminded of how unpredictably consequential their sounds were. When he'd lived with his family, the humans would make any number of sounds, none of which had anything at all to do with him. Then, from out of the fog of inconsequential noise, something meaningful would come: his name would be called, for instance, and a bowl of food that he had left for later would be taken up or a doorbell would sound, someone would shout, and he, clearly the only one who cared about these sporadic invasions of their territory, would have to bark at the intruder or jump up on it to make certain it was submissive and no threat to any of them.

As he ate his rice and chicken livers, Majnoun paid attention to the humans, ready to eat faster if they reached down for the plate.

– What a good eater! said the woman. What a good dog!

Then, exhausted, Majnoun lay back in the wicker basket. He allowed the man to rub him with foul-smelling goo and refasten the cone. He was asleep by the time they left him alone.

It was six months before Majnoun could stand up for more than a few minutes at a time. Even then, he could not use the back leg whose tendons had been most damaged. For a long time, he was essentially three-legged. Also, it was humiliating to be unable to shit and piss outside. The humans made it even worse by putting under-pants on him. They changed him regularly, but not always as quickly as he would have liked.

In the months it took him to recover, he had little to do but lie in his bed and think about life: his life, life in general. It pained him to do this, because his thoughts inevitably returned to the night of his betrayal. He had been betrayed by the dog with the crumpled face.

He had spoken his mind and heart, struggling to express himself out of a sense of fraternity. In return, the crumpled-face dog had been among those who'd tried to kill him. And yet, it sometimes seemed to Majnoun that the others had been right to attack him. He had drifted so far from his instincts, it was not clear – even to himself – that he deserved to live as a dog.

For months, the only thing that distracted him from these sometimes painful thoughts were the humans. They fascinated and frustrated him in equal measure. What, if he were called to give an account of humans, would he say about them? Where would he begin? How to define their smells, for instance? Complex: foods and sweat interrupted by unplaceable odours. They generally smelled of unusual things, but the human smell he liked best was when they were mating. It was sharp and true and comforting, so that on some nights, after they'd moved his basket into their bedroom, he slept more peacefully, the smell of their copulating acting as a kind of tranquilizer.

Then, too, he gradually learned more about their language, moving beyond its rudiments. To begin with, he took in the subtleties of tone. For instance, one would speak to the other in a rising voice and then you could feel the expectation until the one who'd been addressed spoke back. The tone seemed to matter more than the words themselves. And it was always a little odd when they used the rising tone with him, as if waiting for a rejoinder, as if they expected him to understand.

– *Are you hungry, Jim?*
– *Want to go outside, Jim?*
– *Is Jimmy cold? Are you cold, Lord Jim?*

In fact, Majnoun's fascination with tone of voice is what led to his first serious contretemps with the woman. He spent most of his time with the woman. She seemed the more interested in his company, moving his basket from the bedroom to a room with a large desk. She'd spend hours at the desk, getting up only to stretch or to speak to him or to bring a cup from the kitchen. One day, she rose from the desk, stretched, wandered to his basket, scratched his head and said

– Are you hungry, Jim? Would you like a treat?

Majnoun thought about it, then said

– Yes.

Though the sound *yes* was difficult for him to produce, he had been practising it for himself, along with the sound *no* and any number of other significant words. He had also practised nodding, to indicate assent, and shaking his head from left to right to indicate dissent. When the woman asked if he wanted a treat, he was not certain which was more effective: the nod of assent or the spoken 'yes.' For a few moments after saying 'yes,' he was still not certain, because the woman was immobile, staring at him. Confused by her reaction, Majnoun looked her in the eyes, nodded and then said again

– Yes.

The woman began breathing quickly, then fell to the floor. She did not move for several minutes. Unsure what was expected of him – he had never encountered this sudden human immobility – Majnoun lowered his head, licked the fur on his paw and waited to see what would happen. After a while, the woman stirred, mumbling to herself. Then she got up. Perhaps, thought Majnoun, she's unsure if she understood me right. He looked up at her, nodded and said

– Treat.

This time, she cried out and ran from the room in terror. It occurred to Majnoun that what he had taken for straightforward – the rising tone, the appropriate response – was a more complicated transaction than he'd surmised. Certainly, when the man had said the word *yes* or the word *treat*, the woman had not run from *him*. Perhaps, he thought, there was some subtle, accompanying sound that he'd missed: a click of the tongue, a whine, a small growl. He could not recall having heard the man make such sounds. At most, the man put an arm around her shoulder when speaking. Perhaps, then, he ought to have touched her before saying 'yes'?

Next time, thought Majnoun, I'll touch her shoulder if she leans down.

What followed was so unpleasant, however, that there was to be no 'next time' for a very long time indeed. The consequences of his having spoken were clear: the woman was now frightened of him. She would not enter any room he happened to be in. Then the man took Majnoun to a place where he was left overnight. The following day, Majnoun was prodded, poked, given needles, fed food that did not taste proper and kept for observation in a cage beside other dogs who grew aggressive at the smell of him. *This* was humanity, this unpredictability, this cruel behaviour and bullying. The worst of it was, in his weakened state, he could not open the door to his cage. He had no choice but to attend his fate.

The whole business provided a good, if unexpected, lesson. He would almost certainly have tried to communicate with cats or squirrels, mice or birds, if he could make out their language. He might have tried to communicate with *any* species. From that moment on, however, he resolved to hide his knowledge of human language from humans themselves. It was evident that, for whatever reason, humans could not stand to be spoken to by dogs.

On the third day, the woman returned for him herself.

Just as Majnoun was settling into sleep, the other dogs having grown tired of threatening him, the door to the room opened and the woman was led in by one of the men who'd held him down so that a man in white could take some of his blood. The man opened the door to his cage and, not without trepidation, Majnoun followed the woman out.

Once on the street, it occurred to Majnoun that he ought to run for it. The evening was inviting. It was late spring. The sun had not quite set. A reddish strand lay over the buildings in the distance. But, of course, Majnoun was still hampered by his injuries, by the pain he experienced when running. He could not have run for long and he would only have exhausted himself or, worse, got himself lost in territory he did not know. So he climbed into the back seat of the car.

Rather than go to the driver's seat, the woman climbed in the back with him.

— I'm sorry I sent you to that place, she said, but you frightened me. Do you understand?

Resigned to whatever would come, but firm in his resolve not to speak human words, Majnoun nodded.

— What are you? she asked. Are you a dog?

A surprisingly difficult question to answer. He did not feel very much like a dog. He felt adrift between species. But he knew what she meant by the word, so again he nodded.

— You have to understand, she said, that dogs never speak to people. It's never happened, as far as I know. I thought you were possessed. That's why I was frightened. What's your name?

This Majnoun would not say, not only because 'Majnoun,' the name his master had given him, was difficult for him to pronounce, not only because he would not speak, but also because it seemed to him that he no longer had a true name. He stared at the woman, then shook his head.

— My name is Nira, she said. Do you mind if I call you Jim?

An impossible question. Majnoun was unsure what Nira wanted to know. Did he accept the name 'Jim'? Yes, why not? Did he feel displeasure at the thought that she would use the name 'Jim' when referring to him? No, he did not. He stared at her and then, guessing at the appropriate signal, nodded his head.

— You're never going to speak to me again, are you? Nira asked.

Another difficult question. He did not intend to use human words, but as far as he was concerned he *was* speaking to her. This time, he did not answer. He turned to look out the window at the lamplit park on the other side of the street.

— Never mind, said Nira. It's my fault. You don't have to speak if you don't want to.

In all the time they spent together before Majnoun spoke again, Nira never asked him to speak. In fact, she grew to admire his wordlessness. Majnoun rarely barked. He could see no point in using a language he knew Nira did not understand. He communicated all of his needs and most of his thoughts with a nod or a shake of the head. And as they grew closer, Nira needed even less from him. She learned to read his expression, the disposition of his body, the tilt of his head.

At that moment, however, the two sitting in the back of the Honda Civic, it was not obvious that they would develop anything like 'understanding' or 'friendship.' Nira was still frightened of Majnoun. Yes, he was obviously hobbled, unable to walk for long without stopping and lying down, and his limitations called forth her pity. It's why they'd taken him in, after finding him clinging to life in High Park. But the thought that an intelligent being was in their home, that she had let this creature into her bedroom, into the very heart of her private life ... the thought was as humiliating as it was frightening. It took her a long time to overcome these feelings. Majnoun never again slept in her bedroom, for instance, and she ever after felt embarrassed whenever she came upon him licking his genitals.

What helped bind the two was the quality of Majnoun's silence. It was sophisticated, the kind of silence that invited response. Nira spoke to him, at first, about trivial things: work, home renovations, the minor annoyances of living with her husband, Miguel. Gradually, she began to open up about deeper matters: her thoughts about life and death, her feelings about other humans, her concerns for her own well-being – she had survived a bout of cancer and was, at times, helplessly afraid of its return.

Though Majnoun was neither smarter nor quicker than she was, Nira gave him credit for a wisdom she supposed must come from his unique vantage on the world. But it did not always occur to her that Majnoun's vantage also limited his ability to imagine or understand her concerns. For instance, when she complained that her husband was terribly untidy, that he had the disgusting habit of cutting his toenails and biting the clippings, Majnoun looked at her, utterly perplexed. It seemed to him that Miguel was right to groom himself this way. Did she wish to bite Miguel's clippings herself, he wondered.

On another occasion, while he lay in his wicker basket, she asked
– Do you believe in God?

Majnoun had never heard the word before. He'd tilted his head, as if to ask her to repeat the question. And she did her best to explain the concept behind the word. As Majnoun took it, the word seemed to refer to a 'master of all masters.' Did he believe in such a being? The thought had never occurred to him, but he supposed such a being was possible. So, when she asked the question again, he nodded to say 'yes.' This was not the answer she wanted.

– How can you believe such a ridiculous thing? she asked. I suppose you believe God is a dog?

Majnoun believed no such thing. He believed only that the 'god' Nira had described was possible, the same way that he believed a bitch perpetually in heat was possible. A 'master of all masters' was an idea, but it was one that did not concern him, so he could not understand Nira's contempt. They had similar misunderstandings when they spoke of 'government' (a group of masters deciding how a pack should behave) and 'religion' (a group of masters deciding how a pack should behave toward a master of masters). The more Nira spoke of these things, the more difficult it was for Majnoun to believe that any group of masters – especially human ones – could act in concert, whatever the purpose or end. So that both 'government' and 'religion' began to seem like very bad ideas.

Perhaps the most frustrating moment – for both of them – came when Nira asked if he had ever loved another dog. As with *god*, Majnoun had no idea what the word *love* meant. Nira did her best over several days to give him a sense of the word's meaning, but Majnoun found her definitions contradictory, frustrating and vague. The word corresponded to no emotion he could recognize, but her ideas were intriguing enough to keep him attentive. For her part, Nira was convinced that any animal as sensitive as Majnoun *must* have felt love.

– The feeling you had for your mother, she said, that's one of the meanings of *love*.

But if Majnoun had ever known his mother, it had been too brief an acquaintance to stimulate any specific emotion. Nor were there likelier candidates for Majnoun's love. His master? His master had been a master, and one was loyal to masters out of habit, fear, or necessity. Certainly, Majnoun had enjoyed his time as a pup. He was grateful for his master. At the thought of him, Majnoun recalled moments of sheer pleasure chasing a ball thrown in a patchy field, inexpressible joy. But where his master was concerned, Majnoun's emotions were more complex and much darker than 'love,' encompassing as they did feelings of resentment and dislike. No, if he had to choose a human word, Majnoun would have chosen *loyalty* to express what he felt for his master. (For this reason, despite feeling nameless, he'd have preferred Nira call him Majnoun, the name his master had given him.)

For other dogs he'd felt no emotion as complex as loyalty, let alone the emotion Nira was trying to describe. As far as Majnoun was concerned, his relationship to other dogs had been, for the most part, *un*complicated. There were dogs one could dominate and dogs one could not. As other dogs could bite you or mount you when you didn't want it, it was best to keep one's feelings clear and easily communicable.

After a while, Majnoun became convinced that when Nira spoke about 'love,' she was talking about something that was and would always be beyond him. When, one day, she said

– Miguel is my mate. I love him

Majnoun was too bored by the question to be interested. To get Nira to stop asking about 'love,' he nodded his head 'yes' when next she asked if he understood. Both of them knew, however, that he was lying. (As it happened, Majnoun was a poor liar, accompanying as he did his lies with unusual enthusiasm.) And it was a sore point between them.

By the time Nira and Majnoun came to this contretemps about 'love,' eight months had passed and already a thousand intimacies tied them together. She knew what he liked to eat. He knew not to disturb her when she was doing her work. He helped her clean the house as best he could, learning where things went and putting them in their place when he could. She made certain the chew toys he liked best were in good nick, buying new ones whenever the old were too mangled to be enjoyed. In other words, by their eighth month together, Nira and Majnoun were friends.

Also, after eight months, Majnoun could walk without too much pain and even, if he had to, run for short bursts. His worst leg's tendons had healed sufficiently, though he avoided putting all his weight on them. His bandages had long gone and aside from his right ear – the top of which had been chewed clean off by Max – he looked more or less like a normal poodle.

Miguel suggested that Majnoun and Nira should take longer walks together, now that Majnoun was better. He suggested they walk in High Park, but this suggestion was, of course, awkward. Although Nira did not hide Majnoun's sensitivity from her husband, and although he often witnessed the two of them in their version of *causerie*, Miguel did not believe Majnoun could communicate with Nira or she with him, not in any profound way. He assumed, rather, that Majnoun understood a handful of words, but that, beyond these words, the dog simply nodded or shook his head more or less at random. When Nira had first informed him – terrified – that the dog had spoken to her, he had laughed. He couldn't help himself. This dog-and-human communication business was, to his mind, an aspect of Nira's 'granola and Wiccan' tendencies, the same tendencies that had led her to read Mary Daly, to experiment with lesbianism and to speak of the sacredness of her poumpoum. Certainly the dog was bright, but not bright in the human sense, not possessed of great memory or the capacity for speech. So, Miguel did not for an instant consider the emotional complications of High Park.

Some of High Park's complications were trivial; some had psychological weight. On the trivial end: Nira did not know what to do about leashes. There were whole areas of the park where dogs were not allowed to walk about unleashed. She thought it degrading to parade Majnoun about as if he were, well, a dog. Majnoun himself had no opinion on the matter. It did not humiliate him to wear a collar, but he clearly saw the disadvantage of being restrained when aggressive dogs came at him. So they agreed he would have a leash attached to a green leather collar by thin threads. At his slightest jump, the threads would break and Majnoun could stand his ground to defend himself.

(Inherent in the question of leashes was, of course, the question of power. Nira was uncomfortable with power or even with the appearance of it. One day, she asked Majnoun if he would put *her* on a leash, their positions being reversed. He had answered 'no,' and this had made Nira feel even more uncomfortable. But Majnoun had, in fact, misunderstood her question. If she had said

— *Masters have agreed that their submissives must be bound to them with leashes and collars. If you were a master, would you keep me on a leash?*
Majnoun would, without hesitation, have answered 'yes.' If she had been his submissive, he would naturally have treated her according to the custom. Order in a pack is maintained through convention, and it made no sense, as far as Majnoun was concerned, to overturn conventions that worked. But he had understood her question on a more practical level. He had thought of how awkward it would be for him to hold a leash in his mouth while Nira walked about on her hands and knees. Understanding the question as he had, the only possible answer had been the 'no' he'd given.)

Another trivial complication had to do with humans. The humans who came to the park were a varied lot: all stations, races and genders. Inevitably, as Majnoun was striking in his bearing, someone asked Nira if they could touch him or give him treats – the desiccated biscuits, most of which Majnoun found bland and sweet. Nira assumed that Majnoun would not mind the displays of affection. So, she was surprised to discover that, *au contraire*, Majnoun was highly selective in whom he allowed to touch him. Nira would say

— No, he doesn't bite

or

— Sure. I don't think he minds being petted.

And the first few times, he stood still for it. Then, as if for no reason, he decided he'd had enough. An older woman approached and asked if she could pet him and he shook his head 'no.' He moved away at her approach and would not let himself be touched.

– I'm sorry, said Nira.

When the woman had gone on her way, she said to Majnoun

– I didn't know you objected. Don't you like to be touched?

Majnoun shook his head, and that, you'd have thought, was that. Except that it wasn't. From then on, Majnoun decided for himself whom he would allow to touch him, nodding when he was prepared to be touched, shaking his head when he was not.

When Nira was asked

– May I pet your dog?

she answered

– You'll have to ask him yourself.

Questioned, Majnoun would either nod 'yes,' to the delight of the stranger who would then ask

– How did you teach him to do that?

or Majnoun would shake his head 'no,' which was also delightful to strangers and provoked the same question:

– How did you teach him to do that?

Either way, Nira's answer to the question was a shrug of the shoulders.

It being impossible for her to detect any pattern to Majnoun's yeses or nos, she assumed his choices were random. They were not, though his criteria were just beyond Nira's ken. First, Majnoun did not like to be touched by humans who smelled unpleasantly. It was, in human terms, like being asked to shake the hand of someone with shit on his fingers. Second, and more subtly, was the question of station. Versed as he was in the finer aspects of dominance, he recognized at once when someone – for instance, the older woman whose touch was the first he refused – behaved as if they dominated Nira. It was in the old woman's tone, energy and disposition. As Majnoun found it inadmissible that any creature outside his pack (his pack being himself, Miguel and Nira) was of higher status than Nira, he refused to be touched by those who, however inadvertently or unconsciously, belittled her.

In the end, however, High Park's most significant complication was in what it evoked for Majnoun. It was the place where he had almost died. So, naturally, before they went together, Nira had asked if he wished to return to High Park. The name 'High Park' had meant nothing to him, but she made certain he knew it was the place where she and Miguel had found him more dead than alive. She worried that it would be unpleasant for him to recall his trauma, but Majnoun had wanted to return. So they had gone together, and he, to his own surprise, had suffered horribly. The memory of being done almost to death was humiliating. It was also frightening. Nira made a point of avoiding the place where she and Miguel had found him, but that made no difference. Majnoun knew the park well – its smells, its grasses, its hills, its fountains, its roads, its zoo, its restaurants and garbage bins – and it cut him to walk in what had been his territory.

And yet, despite the evident distress it caused him, Majnoun needed High Park.

One day, wishing to spare him the pain, Nira had taken him to Trinity-Bellwoods. Majnoun had looked around and then walked back to the car on his own, waiting for Nira to take him where he wished to go. What he could not communicate was his need to find his former pack or the remnants of it. For reasons he did not himself understand, it was unbearable to think that he might be the last of his kind. The feeling was beyond loneliness. It was desolation. When he was in High Park, Majnoun was both wary *and* hopeful that he would meet his former den mates.

The one Majnoun met at last, Benjy, was not the dog you'd have thought would survive Atticus's reign. But Benjy was resourceful and dishonest in ways Majnoun did not fathom. The dog lied whenever it suited him. He was ingratiating, two-faced, self-interested and, crucially, sensitive. He could read a situation quickly and quickly tell which side of any conflict it was best to be on. He had flaws but his instincts were acute, almost infallible.

That the two met again was pure chance. Majnoun did not like to walk along the road reserved for humans and their dogs. On this road – a depression or narrow valley between modest hills – dogs ran about unleashed. If they were at all aggressive, the dogs would run straight at Majnoun, attacking without warning. Majnoun defended himself very well, however. He was merciless when attacked, having learned a lesson from Atticus, Max, Frick and Frack. In a number of cases he had seriously hurt the attacking dog. He had, for instance, bitten clean through the throat of a Rottweiler, sitting still until it jumped at him, then ruthlessly attacking the dog's underside. The Rottweiler's owner, furious, had run to protect his animal, but by then the Rottweiler was in shock and copiously bleeding. Majnoun, vigilant and wary, had sat beside Nira as the humans shouted at each other.

In a way, Majnoun's attackers were useful. He was not afraid of the dogs who went for him, and his self-confidence grew at each victory. Still, he did not like to hurt other dogs, so he and Nira avoided the off-leash area. One would have thought that the other members of Majnoun's pack would have avoided it as well, the attention of humans or dogs being unwanted. Yet Benjy and Majnoun found each other again near the first of the small bridges over the freshet that ran beside the off-leash road.

How Majnoun got there is easy enough: he was distracted by Nira's talk about the government in some faraway place. It was winter – more than a year after Majnoun had been rescued – and the smell of the world was less sharp, masked by snowfall. So Majnoun (and Nira) wandered into the area without realizing where they were. Benjy, on the other hand, was there out of desperation. He was fleeing, as best he could with his short legs, the attentions of an aggressive Dalmatian.

Benjy saw Majnoun first and cried out in their shared language.
– Black dog! Black dog, help me!

Majnoun looked up to see Benjy half-running, half-tumbling down the hillside.

Immediately, instinctively, Majnoun went to the beagle's aid. To Nira's dismay, Majnoun put himself between the Dalmatian and the beagle, barking and growling as if he were ferocious and unhinged. The Dalmatian thought about challenging Majnoun, but it was now faced with something beyond its comprehension: two dogs that did not feel like dogs, two manifestly alien versions of the canine. With surprising grace, the dog fled back up the hill whence it had come.

– Jim, said Nira, what are you doing?

Majnoun ignored her. He waited for Benjy to recover from his run, then said

– You are the small dog with long ears from our pack.

– Yes, said Benjy. I am that dog. I tell you, black dog, I've been mounted more often than a bitch in heat since those days.

Then, changing the subject, Benjy said

– Have you found a new master? This one does not seem cruel. Does it beat you?

– No, said Majnoun. She is a human I live with and she does not beat me.

– Then you've had good fortune since you left us. I wish you and the dog who spoke strangely had taken me with you.

– I was bitten and left for dead, said Majnoun. I did not choose exile.

– Just what I thought, said Benjy. The others dogs believed you and the strange dog had gone away, but I did not believe it. Why would the black dog leave his den mates, I asked.

– Where are the others? asked Majnoun.

– That would take a lot of words, said Benjy, and I am hungry.

Benjy looked over at Nira. Without warning, he barked happily and rolled over in the snow.

– What are you doing? asked Majnoun.

– It is a thing humans like, said Benjy. Don't you do it? It is a very good way to get food.

– Where are the others? Majnoun repeated.

Again, Benjy barked happily and rolled over in the snow.

– Stop that, said Majnoun. She does not understand your ...

Nira *did* seem to understand, however. She had, with a kind of fascination, been watching the two. She was hearing what she thought of as Majnoun's real language for the first time: clacks, low growls, rough barks, sighs and yawns. It was incomprehensible. The only part that made sense to her was Benjy's playful barking and his rolling over in the snow. So, interrupting Majnoun, she said

– Your friend is hungry, isn't he? Why don't we bring him home with us for a while? I didn't bring anything with me to eat, but there's more than enough at home.

Despite himself, Majnoun was annoyed. But, to Benjy, he said

– She says there is food where we live.

– You understand human language? asked Benjy. I would like you to teach me. If you teach me, I'll tell you everything you want to know about our pack.

– You'll tell me what I want to know or I'll bite your face, said Majnoun.

But Majnoun was a poor liar in both of his languages, and Benjy was not troubled. Benjy, who *was* a good liar, had seen Majnoun's body after Atticus, Max and the brothers had finished with it, and having seen Majnoun 'dead,' he was not frightened of him. He assumed that if Atticus and his co-conspirators had got the better of Majnoun, he could almost certainly outsmart Majnoun as well. Why should he respect a dog who was demonstrably inferior to Atticus?

He went home with Nira and Majnoun, blithely.

No sooner did Nira put down a bowl of rice and chicken livers than the beagle was on it, eating as if afraid Majnoun would take some. He had not had anything proper to eat in days. He'd had no luck begging from humans along Bloor Street. So he'd returned to High Park, searching for scraps beneath the snowfall and, even, hunting for the mice and rats that scampered around the restaurant near the dog park.

Winter was not a good season for a dog without a master. Alone, Benjy spent most of his time going from house to house looking for someone to take him in, doing the things humans – mysteriously, incomprehensibly – liked dogs to do. He rolled over, pretended to be dead, sat up, stood on his hind legs (which was difficult for him), begged for food and, on occasion, howled in imitation of human song. When one thought about it, a dog had to take it on faith that humans possessed intelligence. They were expert makers of dens and food, however, and those were the things Benjy wanted from them. Clearly, he could get them more efficiently if he learned human language.

– You know, said Benjy after he'd finished eating and drinking, I always thought you were the most clever dog. I am certain that's why the pack leader wanted to kill you.

– The grey dog with the cascading face? asked Majnoun.

The two were in the living room, on their own. Nira, feeling as if she were intruding on Majnoun's privacy, left them alone for a time. The living room had a brightly coloured throw rug – crimson, light straw and gold – on its floor. It had an armchair and a sofa, a false fireplace and windows that looked onto the street, windows Majnoun could look out of, if he sat on the sofa.

Benjy ignored Majnoun's question.

– It does not surprise me, he said, that you have learned to speak with humans. I would be your submissive, if you would teach me a little of what you know.

Majnoun was looking out the window at the passing world: cars, pedestrians, other dogs and the cats whose appearance always made him growl. He knew it was senseless to dislike the poor, weak creatures, but he could not help himself and often found – to his own dismay – that it was difficult to suppress the desire to bark at the sight of felines. As Benjy said 'teach me,' a cat passed near enough to the house to provoke a growl. Thinking Majnoun's growl was meant for him, Benjy said

– I am an innocent dog. I have not done you any wrong.

Getting down from the sofa, the window proving too much of a distraction, Majnoun said

— I will teach you human words if you tell me where the others are.

— The others, said Benjy, are dead. I thought I was the last of our pack.

Although there was no real need for Benjy to hide what had happened to the pack, he was wary of saying too much. For one thing, he had been responsible for the pack's demise and he was not sure how Majnoun would react if he knew. So, in his retelling, Benjy left out any detail that might incriminate him, while adding little flourishes here and there to make himself look better than he had been. These flourishes and silences did not misrepresent the character of Atticus's reign, however. Benjy, essentially, told the truth.

He had been awake for the killing of Athena. He had seen Frick make off with her body and had watched as Frack roused Bella and led her away. It didn't take much thought to guess Bella's fate. What took thought was the decision their deaths forced on him: should he stay or leave? If Frick and Frack were willing to kill so wantonly, why wouldn't they kill him? He would be little more trouble to them than Athena had been. On the other hand, exile was a frightening idea. What would life be without the bigger dogs around to defend him? His only course would be to find a master and, humans being dangerous, this was not something he wanted to do.

The other thing that was clear on the night of Athena's murder was who the conspirators were. Frick, Frack, Max and Atticus had been furtive from early on, at times keeping to themselves. So, when Frick and then Frack had gone off, Benjy had turned to where Max was lying. He had turned and waited. He waited until the strange disappearance of Prince and then observed the stealthy commotion as the brothers and Max searched the den. When the conspirators had left the den, Benjy had followed, going to a tree a distance away from the coppice. He hid in a place that was far enough from the den to afford him some safety but close enough so that he could observe the comings and goings. It was from here that he heard the terrifying fracas that signalled the attack on Majnoun.

Now, the mystery deepened for him. The conspirators had gone after Majnoun, Bella, Athena and Prince. Where was the logic? What connected the four who had been disposed of? More importantly, as far as Benjy was concerned, where did *he* fit in the scheme of things? Was there something that tied him to the victims, or was he connected to the conspirators?

Once the conspirators had returned to the coppice, Benjy sought out the body of Majnoun, saw that the dog was to all appearances dead, and peed on what he took to be the corpse, marking it so that others might be wary of him, if they connected his scent with this violence. After that, still uncertain about what he should do, but convinced he could flee if he had to, Benjy returned to the coppice where, to his surprise, all the dogs were asleep. Warily, he went to his place and stayed there until morning.

In the morning, a new order came with the sunlight. The dogs woke early, two of them – that is, Bobbie and Dougie – confused by a difference they could not understand.

– Where is the big bitch? asked Bobbie.

Atticus yawned before he snapped his jaws together. Then, he barked while Frick and Frack nosed Bobbie, Dougie and Benjy toward him.

– These are the last words I'll speak in this useless tongue, said Atticus. The dogs who have not wanted to stay with us have gone into exile. The big bitch has died. Humans have taken her body away. I am now the leader of this pack. Does any dog object?

– You will make a wonderful leader, said Benjy.

– Whether I am wonderful or not, I will lead. Those who wish can choose exile. Those who stay will live properly, like dogs. We don't need words for doors or trees. We don't need to talk about time or hills or stars. We did not talk about those things before, and our ancestors did well without this language. From now on, anyone who speaks anything but the old tongue will be punished. We will hunt. We will defend our territory. The rest does not concern us.

– I cannot stop the words that go on inside me, said Bobbie.

– No one can stop that, said Atticus. Keep them inside.

– And if we speak by mistake? asked Dougie.

– You will be punished, said Atticus.

Who knows why, in these circumstances, a dog would speak up. Benjy was too busy taking it all in. How, he wondered, would they be punished for speaking? How was Atticus to stop them from speaking with each other when they were alone? And why the injunction in the first place? Their language gave them an advantage over other dogs. Still, thought Benjy, might does what might will do, whether it was humans beating you for pissing or Atticus insisting that dogs should not speak. It was best to let those in power do what they wished while finding some advantage in it for oneself.

Evidently, the orange bitch did not see things his way.

– I choose exile, said Bobbie.

– We will help you leave, answered Atticus.

As if it had been worked out in advance, the conspirators attacked the orange bitch at once. They were ruthless and, as the Duck Toller was smaller than any of the four, they did immediate, severe damage. Desperate because she understood they meant to kill her, Bobbie cried out in distress. The sound was terrifying. She managed to run from the den, but the four pursued her, biting at her legs as she ran. They chased her beyond the pond where, weakened, she fell. There, they bit her until her body stopped moving and her blood ran onto the grass.

(While recounting this moment to Majnoun, Benjy was as solemn as could be, as if relating an injustice. The truth was, though, that he had felt admiration for the conspirators. Some part of him admired the four dogs still. They had been swift and clear, and one had to admit that clarity, however terrifying it might be, was at least admirable. It was perhaps even beautiful. He could only aspire to it. It was an ideal that, realistically speaking, a dog of his size and stature could never attain, clarity being an expression of power.)

The murder of the orange bitch was a signal event. After that, it was clear to all that Atticus was serious and that the conspirators wanted what Atticus wanted. It was also clear that the conspirators were a different kind of creature. The attack itself had been ruthless, swift and canine. Admirable, as Benjy thought. But what had preceded it, the offer of exile: why propose such a thing if it were not meant? The orange bitch had taken them at their word and they had murdered her. Why? Benjy could not see the advantage. The bitch had been no threat at all. To him, the decision to kill her had been perverse. And, in the end, it was this perversity that proved the conspirators' strangeness.

As far as Benjy was concerned, Atticus, being unpredictable, was a danger to them all.

On top of that, with the death of Bobbie, it was clear that he and Dougie were now of lowest status. They were meant, it seemed, to scavenge and to be submissive. This was not necessarily a bad thing. Submissiveness was worth the trouble if one's submission were rewarded by something valuable: protection, say. It remained to be seen, however, what good would come from Atticus's reign.

(How quickly the dead pass from mind. Though they had been pack mates, neither Benjy nor Majnoun remembered much about Bobbie, save that her fur had been orange and shaggy and that she had smelled of pine even before they found the coppice. She had once defended Benjy from a mutt that attacked without warning but Benjy did not remember this. At her death, Bobbie imagined she was sinking in deep water, the sensation bringing her back to a moment as a pup when she had nearly drowned. She died in great distress, unconsoled.)

The first days of Atticus's rule were exceedingly peculiar. Dougie was bitten hard when he inadvertently spoke in the new tongue. Thereafter, Dougie and Benjy were careful never to use words when the others were around. They barked. But this was disorienting. They were forced to imitate what they remembered of their old language. They were, in effect, dogs imitating dogs. This would have been less troubling if the imitation had been done for humans. Most humans cannot tell a benign growl from a growl that prefigures attack. Atticus, however, having demanded that the pack return to the old ways, now constantly judged how Benjy and Dougie were performing 'as dogs.' This made everything stranger still. Benjy and Dougie were dogs forced to perform a version of dogness convincing enough to please other dogs who had, to an extent, forgotten what dogness was. Were *any* of them actually barking or growling in the old way? Neither Benjy nor Dougie ever knew. Nor, of course, could they ask. They would have been bitten – or worse – if they had. Far from becoming more doglike, Benjy could feel himself becoming less so: more self-conscious, more thoughtful, more dependent on a language that he kept to himself. The safest thing was to imitate Atticus as best as one could.

In the beginning, Benjy and Dougie were protected when they went scavenging. One or two of the conspirators always went with them, attacking the occasional dog who stood up to them, watching as the smaller dogs got into places the bigger ones could not. At least for Benjy, it was a relief to discover that there was some purpose to his presence in the pack. He and Dougie were adroit finders of things humans had rejected. During their winter in High Park, the two were especially useful. It was rare for the larger dogs to be admitted to a human home, but Dougie and Benjy could sometimes charm their way in and steal useful things: discarded cushions, pieces of foam, old clothes, a moth-eaten blanket left in a yard, anything to make the coppice more hospitable.

After a while, the conspirators, either through laziness or unconcern, allowed the small dogs to go off on their own so that, as might have been expected, the relationship between Benjy and Dougie evolved into a friendship. At first, Benjy could not stand the schnauzer. The thing he felt most like doing, when he and Dougie were together, was to mount him. Not because he wanted to fuck Dougie. No, the desire to dominate when he himself was dominated was strong and instinctive and belonged to the unquellable depths of himself. At the same time, it was obvious that Dougie also wanted to mount *him*. None of this was personal. He wished Dougie no ill, and Dougie almost certainly wished him none. Each simply wanted to get on top of the other. And yet it was personal, too. At times, they fought bitterly over who had the right to mount whom. Their disagreements did not, however, affect the others. All of the others, including Rosie, mounted Benjy and Dougie as a matter of course. And both of them bore this because they had to.

Though the coppice was as hospitable as the dogs could make it, the winter in High Park was just short of disaster. The trees and bushes were adequate windbreaks, but the cold was so often unbearable the small dogs were forced to consider escape. One January night, Benjy wondered if he were going to die, so violent were his shivers, so loud the clacking of his teeth. The following morning, he and Dougie set out early, on their own. The other dogs were all asleep. Atticus, Max, the brothers and Rosie lay together on blankets in a warm congregation from which both Benjy and Dougie had been unceremoniously excluded.

On the January morning of their escape, the snow was almost impassable. The familiar world of smells and sounds and landmarks was lost beneath the snowfall. It seemed to the two as if some strange being had taken everything they knew, leaving only whiteness and the indistinct profile of a world they had once known. When they were far enough from the den, Dougie said

— I'm cold. I thought I was going to die.

— Me too, Benjy said. The others do not think about us.

— I believe you, said Dougie. I tried to sleep next to them and the leader bit me. It isn't right for dogs not to care about dogs.

— They don't want us, now that the ground isn't what it was. They would let us die.

— I believe you, said Dougie. What can we do?

— I am going to find a human to let me in. Why don't we see if there are humans who will take us both?

— Should we tell the others we are going?

— No, answered Benjy. I do not know what would happen.

— I believe you, said Dougie. The leader is strange. It is difficult to know when he will bite, and he bites hard. It will be better if we go on our own.

This decision brought them immediate good fortune. Making their way out of the park by Wendigo Pond, Dougie and Benjy trudged through the snow along Ellis Park Road. There, they were seen and hailed by an old woman.

— Here, doggies! Here, doggies!

Both recognized the tone but they were wary. For as many kindnesses as they'd had from perky summoners, there had been bewildering cruelties: stones thrown, beatings with sticks. They were desperate, however. They were cold and hungry. So they made their way toward her. A good choice, as it happened, because the woman had recently lost two of her six cats and her innate sympathy for all animals was heightened. When they entered her kitchen, she set down two bowls of cat food. And though the food smelled like fish and cinders, it was good.

That winter, Dougie and Benjy had shelter. They were well-fed and they were let out into a yard whenever they liked. The woman and her cats, however, were a kind of trial they endured together. To take the cats first: yes, Benjy and Dougie felt an antipathy toward the creatures. As far as Benjy was concerned, no reasonable being could feel otherwise. He was prepared to live in peace, but the cats that slunk about the old woman's home were more pernicious than the usual felines: hissing constantly, arching their backs as if making themselves bigger could intimidate, jumping up and down with their claws out. They would not live in peace.

In other circumstances, Benjy and Dougie would have ganged up on the pink-tongued hysterics and broken their necks for them. It was clear from the old woman's behaviour, however, that she actually valued the cats. She cleaned up their feces (which, as it happened, tasted very good), groomed them, purred at them or with them as if she were an oversized moggie herself. It was easy to see that if they hurt any of her furry charges she would throw them out. So, when the cats were most annoying – mincing about like legislators – he and Dougie permitted themselves only the quietest of growls, intimate warnings that the cats resolutely ignored.

The woman herself was a more complicated irritant. She was human. So, she could be manipulated in a number of ways the small dogs had mastered. When they were hungry, they rolled onto their backs for her or stood up on their hind legs, a thing she seemed to particularly enjoy. She was inexplicably delighted by certain things but just as inexplicably horrified by others. She petted them and made high-pitched sounds when they jumped into the bed beside her or licked her face, but she would lower her voice and squirt them with water if she caught them licking their own or each other's genitals. She would offer them food whenever they turned on the television for her, but she could not stand to see them eat the cats' droppings.

Her unpredictable likes and dislikes were not the worst of her. The worst of her was her clinginess. The two had encountered this particular fetish before, of course. Both knew what it was like to have a human hold you for too long: the suffocation, the back-cracking struggle to get away. But the woman seemed to have some need to crush them. She held them tight no matter how they squirmed.

One day, Dougie asked

– Do you think she could kill us when she squeezes?

Benjy found it troubling that he could not answer one way or the other. He had no idea if the old lady was a hazard, no way of knowing. And it seemed unwise to depend on the restraint of a being one did not know. On top of that, there was the feeling that accompanied the crush. It was as if the woman were trying to instill something in them or to communicate a thought. Gradually, over the last of winter and the beginning of spring, she became unbearable. By the first warm days, Benjy and Dougie found themselves again dreaming of escape; this, despite the food and shelter the woman provided.

Dougie first spoke of his desire to leave, on an evening when the world smelled again of things expunged by winter: muck, greenery, rotten food and shit. He and Benjy were in the woman's yard, lying on the warm patio stones. Dougie had had enough of the old woman and of the cats who polluted her den.

— This is not where I want to be, he said.

— Where will you go if you leave? asked Benjy.

— I want to go where we were, he answered. These creatures are making me unhappy and the human will break me, I'm certain of it.

— It would be dangerous to go back, said Benjy.

— The leader is a true dog, said Dougie. He will teach us how to be true dogs again.

— Going back is an idea that is not good, but I do not want to stay here on my own.

— Then come with me. The world is warm. We can live with our pack, as we were meant to.

Dougie had apparently forgotten the abuse and the humiliations they had suffered. He'd forgotten how frightened they'd been, had forgotten how violent and unpredictable the pack could be. Benjy shared his longing for the company of their pack, but he could not see any profit in a return. He saw only danger and, ever practical, he thought first of what was good for him. As clingy as the old woman was, there had to be alternatives to returning to the coppice.

— Why not find another human? he asked.

— No, Dougie answered. Why change one master for another?

— Their homes are different, said Benjy. They smell different. I believe they *are* different. We may find one who has none of these ugly creatures with them.

— We are from the same pack, said Dougie. I know what you are saying, but my thinking is not like yours. We have a home elsewhere. I want to go back. We can look for another place, if the pack is still strange.

Dougie would not be dissuaded. He no longer wished to live with this human or these cats. His spirit would not allow it. A few days after their talk, he precipitated their ouster from the old woman's house. His behaviour would have terrible consequences, it's true, but Benjy would not blame his friend for the events that followed their ouster. He *could* not. In fact, by the time he told all this to Majnoun, he'd convinced himself that Dougie had been considerate when he'd got them both thrown out of the house. 'Considerate,' in that his actions forced Benjy to reconsider where and how he wanted to live, forcing on him the unexpected dignity of a choice.

First, however, the ouster: Benjy had always been an excellent hunter. He could sniff out rats, knew how to kill them and, from time to time, enjoyed eating them. They were not his preferred meal, so he did not kill them unless he was hungry. Dougie, on the other hand, was a masterful hunter and enjoyed killing rats and mice for the sport. It was, simply, Dougie's way, and Benjy thought nothing of it. That is, he thought nothing of it until Dougie cornered and killed one of the woman's cats.

It happened in a moment that left Benjy feeling profoundly ambivalent. They had been lying together, he and Dougie, in the kitchen, when one of the cats came in and went for its bowl of water. Without warning, Dougie struck. (How fast he was, and how wonderful!) The cat, its reflexes almost as impressive as Dougie's, tried to jump out of Dougie's way, jumping straight up and screeching for its life. To no avail. It was trapped in a narrow vee where the side of a cupboard met a wall. It tried to jump a second time, but it had no chance. Anticipating its desperate movements, avoiding its claws, Dougie darted in, bit the cat's neck and shook it as if it were a plush toy until it stopped wriggling and hung limply in his mouth.

What pleasure it must have given Dougie to do this, thought Benjy. (He judged Dougie's pleasure from the pleasure the spectacle had given *him*.) The sound alone had been arousing: the screeches that were the cat's last pleas, the struggle of the thing in Dougie's mouth as he knocked it against the wall and sunk his teeth in deeper, breaking it almost in two, it seemed, as he shook its corpse. Benjy felt a deep satisfaction at the creature's demise. Dougie had killed one of the haughtiest of the cats, one that hissed and arched its back when either of the dogs was close to its prized possessions: a pink ball of wool, a wicker basket lined with a pink blanket. They had often entertained each other with talk of how they would, someday, bite it to death. That day had come and it was good.

If Benjy had killed the creature, he would have left its body in the kitchen and retired to some other part of the house. He would not have hidden, exactly, but he would not have wanted to be associated with its death. Dougie, however, took the corpse upstairs to the human's bedroom, the cat's head knocking against the struts of the bannister. Benjy did not follow him up. He waited in the living room and listened. He did not have to wait for long, nor did he have to listen intently. He heard Dougie's nails on the hardwood. There was a momentary silence and then the woman began to wail. A further moment passed and, as the woman cried, evidently upset about the cat, Dougie descended the stairs, unhurried, almost thoughtfully.

– What happened? asked Benjy.

– I do not know, answered Dougie. I put the creature down beside her and then she began to make noise.

– Was she displeased?

– No, said Dougie, she seemed frightened.

– Maybe she thought you might do the same thing to her.

– I felt the same, said Dougie. So, I left the creature for her.

– That was wise, said Benjy.

For a long while, the two of them sat in the living room, listening to the sounds of the woman, waiting for her to call them.

(Here, Majnoun interrupted Benjy's account.

– That was not a good thing for the bearded dog to do, he said. Humans protect the creatures. They call them 'cats.'

As Majnoun could not precisely pronounce the word, it came out like the *ch* in the Scottish word *loch* followed by a *t*. It was the sound of something caught in the throat.

– It is a good name for them, said Benjy.)

But the woman did not call them. She descended the stairs carrying the dead cat in her arms as if it were her child, holding its body to her chest.

— What have you done? she said to them. What have you done?

Despite himself, Benjy found the sight exciting. It was so oddly incongruous. And for the first time in his life, a feeling within him was so powerful it forced the low sounds of pure joy from him. In other words, he laughed. Dougie laughed as well, the two of them helplessly releasing the emotion within, as if some container inside them had broken and its contents flooded out. Benjy had released tension before but in very different circumstances and in very different ways. He had, for instance, barked happily when, as a pup, he'd rolled in the green and humid grass of his master's front lawn. *This* laughter was strange, however. It was not provoked by his senses but by something almost as powerful: his intellect.

If laughter was strange for the dogs, the sight (or rather the sound) of it was clearly disturbing to the woman. She stood still at the entrance to the living room, listening to them, the dead cat in her arms. And seeing her there holding the dead cat as if it were precious, Benjy and Dougie were further amused. They could not stop laughing, their low growls like some strange fit. Clutching the dead cat to her chest, the woman got down on her knees, bowed her head, and put her hands together as if she were begging. She did not speak to them, though she was clearly speaking to someone.

After a long while, during which she fervently said whatever it was she had to say, the woman rose, opened the door to her home and moved out of the way.

If it had been up to Benjy, they would have stayed. He could feel the woman's terror and he was certain they could exploit it. (It did trouble him that she was speaking to the unseen.) But Dougie, though he was as struck by the woman's reactions as Benjy, wanted only to get out of the house. He bounded out the door without looking back. So, Benjy followed.

From the moment they left the woman's house, Benjy had premonitions of disaster. They were not far from the den, and he knew the way as well as Dougie, but he followed some distance behind.

Coming up to the coppice, Dougie moved even quicker, happy as he entered what had been their home. There was silence and, moments later, a burst of growls and barking as Dougie ran out again. He was pursued by Atticus and the brothers. The three sounded different – not feral, not domesticated, not like dogs. Benjy was immediately afraid and, bad luck for him, when Dougie ran from the den he ran straight at him, speaking his last words in his first tongue. That is, in his final moments, Dougie unmistakably spoke the universal language of dogs.

– I submit, he yelped. I submit! I submit!

as if he were being done by unknown dogs who, for some reason, could not understand him at all.

Recalling his friend's death, Benjy stopped speaking. Overwhelmed by emotion, he lay down and dropped his head on a crimson patch of carpet.

He and Majnoun were quiet for a long while. Aware of the silence, Nira entered and asked Majnoun if he or his friend wanted anything to eat or drink. At Nira's entrance, Benjy jumped up and began to walk in front of her, back and forth, looking up and barking until Majnoun told him to stop.

In answer to Nira's question, Majnoun shook his head 'no.' So, after turning on the light in the room, Nira again left the dogs alone.

– I'm amazed, said Benjy, that this human treats you so well. You do nothing for it. Do you walk on your hind legs now and then? You must do something.

– I do nothing like that, answered Majnoun.

– This does not sound like the usual master, said Benjy. A master who wants nothing is not a master. And if this is not a master, it will bring you pain. You will suffer one day. It is always better to know with whom you are dealing, don't you agree?

– I understand your thinking, said Majnoun, but this human is not a master. I do not know what Nira is, but I am not afraid.

– 'Nira'? said Benjy. You can speak its name? That is very strange.

— Tell me what happened after the dog was killed, said Majnoun. Why would they kill him if he submitted?

— I think, said Benjy, that they could not help themselves.

Benjy watched as the three dogs bit at Dougie's legs, belly and neck. Dougie struggled to the end, attempting to get away. He was outnumbered, however, by dogs who were single-minded in their attack. Dougie was as spirited and valiant as a dog could be under the circumstances, getting a few bites in himself, but his valour served no purpose, it seemed to Benjy, other than to prolong his suffering.

While Atticus, Frick and Frack were occupied with killing, Benjy backed away from the scene, his tail tucked between his legs. He would have run, but just as he turned to flee, Rosie was on him, bounding out of the den. Catching him by surprise, she had her teeth firmly in his neck before he knew what to do. He peed in submission and went as limp as a pup, but she held on and growled, forcing him to be present at Dougie's death.

(Benjy could not express what he'd felt on watching his friend being killed. Every fibre of him had felt hatred for the three who killed Dougie. He hated them still, as he recounted Dougie's death, but he hid his emotions from Majnoun, thinking them a sign of weakness.)

Once Dougie stopped moving, the three dogs — Atticus and the brothers — stood around his remains, as if waiting for him to get up. Atticus even nudged Dougie's head, pushing him, as if to make certain he was dead or as if hoping he were still alive. For a moment, the killers seemed puzzled by what they'd done. You'd have said they'd come upon Dougie's body, not that they had reduced it to what it was: an unmoving clump from which Dougie's spirit had fled. Their bewilderment — if that is what it was — was brief. Seeing that Dougie's body no longer moved, Atticus and the brothers turned to Benjy.

As they came at him, Benjy assumed his life was through. He made himself as small and unthreatening as he could. But, for some reason, Atticus and the brothers were no longer interested in violence. Atticus looked at Benjy, growled and returned to the coppice. The others followed, leaving Dougie's body to rot where humans would find it.

Were it not for Rosie, Benjy would have fled as soon as the three turned away. But Rosie growled to remind him she was there and nudged him forward as if he had been one of her pups. So, against his will, Benjy returned to life with his own kind or, more accurately, with those he assumed were his own kind. As he quickly came to understand, the pack had changed. They were now almost as mysterious to Benjy as humans were. He felt the same instinctive fear for Atticus as other dogs must have felt for the twelve of them when they had first fled from their cages.

One thing for certain: he no longer belonged in the coppice.

Atticus, the brothers and Rosie still refused to use the new words. But neither did they communicate in the old way – or, at least, what Benjy remembered the old way to be. There were still growls, lowered eyes and exposed necks. But along with that there were strange movements of the head, there was a kind of muzzle-pointing that had nothing to do with indicating direction, there was a stuttered bark that sounded to Benjy like human imitations of barking. Their movements and sounds were now unselfconsciously produced but they were even further away from the canine. The pack had grown very peculiar indeed: an imitation of an imitation of dogs. All that had formerly been natural was now strange. All had been turned to ritual.

Take the business of mounting, for instance.

– I could not move, said Benjy, without one of them biting my neck and fucking me.

In times gone by, mounting had always been an instinctive matter, no more worth thinking about than breathing was. Nor had it always been about status. At times one had an erection, because it was such pleasure to meet other dogs. The lines that separated happiness from fucking and fucking from dominance were fairly clear.

By the time Benjy returned to the pack, however, Atticus and the others mounted him, it seemed, in order to prove that there was order and hierarchy. That is, to prove it to themselves. And for the first time in his life, it occurred to Benjy that being mounted was a humiliation. He understood why the others did it and he would certainly have mounted any dog weaker than himself, but this new feeling, this shame, changed him. He began to think about it.

For instance, it occurred to him one day while Frick was atop him that if the point were to demonstrate that one had the power to mount another, the point did not need to be made over and over. The point being made once or twice, it became obvious or redundant, a mere reflex to which smaller dogs like himself were forced to submit. He submitted without resistance, accepting his place in the echelon. After all, he believed with all his soul that the social order was the most important thing. And yet ...

There came a moment with Rosie, one in which he began to see himself and the pack differently. He and the German shepherd were apart from the others, alone in the coppice. Though Benjy thought of his second stay in the coppice as a long one, it lasted not much more than two months. During that time, there was little communication with Atticus or the brothers. They would not speak to him. He and Rosie, however, sometimes found themselves alone together. One afternoon, she surprised him by using the old (new) tongue.

– You should not try to run away, she said. They will hurt you if you do.

Once he'd recovered from the surprise of being addressed in their old language – and decided to risk speaking back – Benjy asked why dogs should hurt one who wished to be free.

Rather than answer, Rosie told him what had happened to Max. When Benjy and Dougie had fled, the others – Rosie included – began to mount Max. It was only natural, she said, as all of them were superior to the dog. And this was fine, for a while. But then, the dog got it into his head that he should mount one of them. None let him, and what had been balance turned into an unpleasant battle for leadership. It was a battle that escalated until, one winter afternoon, the brothers had had enough. They attacked Max together, leaving him half-dead by the side of the pond. They left it for the leader to finish the dog off, and the leader, naturally, had no choice. It was he who bit through the dog's neck and left him to die.

As far as Rosie was concerned, Max had been to blame for the trouble that led to his death. In killing him, the dogs had behaved according to nature. They had been true dogs: blameless and faithful to the canine. It was up to every dog to follow the right road, to know his place. It was up to Benjy to do so now.

– Do you see? she asked.

He had answered that he did see, but, in fact, he saw more than she did. If he had, previously, wondered why he and Dougie had been kept around, he now had a very good idea: the others needed him, weak and lowly though he was, to maintain their echelon. This thought, which he shared with no one, instilled in him a sense of his own power. He, Benjy, was in his way as necessary as the leader, for if there is a top there must necessarily be a bottom. Why, then, should he alone be mounted? Wasn't it reasonable to think that from time to time the leader should allow himself to be mounted by the lowest – that is, Benjy? The heights depend on the depths. This revolutionary thought, new as it was to him, was disturbing. It was a paradox that Benjy could neither shake nor resolve, and it set him – unconsciously, at first – against his pack mates.

Two months into his time with the others in the coppice, Benjy too began to lose his sense of the canine. He could not piss or sit still without wondering if he were doing it right. The selfconsciousness was disorienting, its effect very like listening to the strange-speaking dog:

> How the sky moves above the world!
> How the ground's fur is changed.
> All to distract the dog with bones,
> buried or dug. He will wander unsatisfied.

So, although Benjy was unsure about many things, he was certain that he wanted no part of Atticus's pack. He had to get away. The thing was, he knew escape would be difficult. He had become a part of the pack's rituals, their necessary underdog. As a result, they kept a close watch on him, protecting him from strange dogs, yes, but ready to pounce if he made the slightest misstep. In the end, it was only through good fortune – good fortune for him, good fortune guided by spite – that Benjy managed to escape. That is, he found a garden of death.

Gardens of death are difficult to speak of. For dogs, they exist only on the edge of awareness. They are the places – sometimes literally gardens – where humans leave poison for animals to eat. For obvious reasons, few living dogs know about them. To begin with, those who discover them seldom live to learn from their discovery. And then, they rarely die within the gardens. Poisoned dogs tend to die well away from the places where they've been poisoned. So, their dead bodies do not serve as warnings to others.

In his life, Benjy – an extremely cautious dog – had, to his knowledge, known but two gardens of death. The first had been three houses away from his master's home. It was a vegetable garden from which there inevitably came enticing smells, smells both mineral and fleshy. All one had to do to enter the garden was to use a dugout that went under the yard's metal fence. Any number of dogs entered and ate. The breath and arses of the ones who did smelled of rust and rubbing alcohol. The smaller ones died soon after their breath took on the smell. The larger ones either died or became very sick. Benjy had free run of the neighbourhood and he had gone into the garden a number of times. There, buried a little way under the ground, you could find cow's meat, pieces of cooked chicken or even sugary breads. It had been tempting to dig the good things up and eat them, but, as well as being naturally suspicious, Benjy was well-fed. He had dug up a bone or two on which there was still much meat, but he'd resisted eating what smelled like mineral flesh. He had, instead, contented himself with sniffing at the dogs, cats and dying raccoons who had not.

Just as the pattern had imposed itself on his memory, just as he'd linked the garden with suffering and death, the ground had ceased to bring those things. The garden was trampled, meats were no longer buried there, and the animals who entered did not grow sick, did not die.

It had all been so odd, so fascinating, that Benjy never forgot either the place or its association with pain and death. And then, on one of his forays to the houses beside the park, he caught the smell of rust and rubbing alcohol on the breath of an agonizing dog whose body writhed in the tall weeds along Parkside Drive. A few evenings later, along Ellis Park Road, he, with Frick and Frack behind him, had passed a house from which came the same strange tang: alcohol and rust. Benjy barked, calling the brothers away from the house to a provocative scent at the base of a willow tree. (The dogs who used the park seemed all to piss vanilla, honey, alfalfa, clover and something not quite definable but entrancing nevertheless.) He was not certain there was a garden of death behind the house, but if there was, he wanted all of Atticus's pack – as he now thought of them – to eat there at once.

It was disturbing to imagine the death of his fellows. His pack would die out: a desolating thought, despite his hatred for the others. Then again, he had no idea what effect the garden of death would have. It was possible that Atticus's pack would merely be incapacitated, allowing him to flee the coppice. In either case, Benjy could see no other route to freedom. All he had to do was lead those who'd killed Dougie to the proper place. The garden itself would do the rest.

The following morning, as they all set out from their den, Benjy drifted toward Ellis Park Road. That is, he made a show of sniffing tree trunks that led in the direction of Ellis Park Road. As if the gods themselves approved of Benjy's intentions, on this summer morning the trees along the way were redolent of fascinating urine. The pack moved inexorably in the direction of the house that had hinted of death.

Benjy worried, as they approached the house on Ellis Park, that the garden would bring neither death nor incapacity, that it would bring mere discomfort. If so, he might well be punished, if they blamed him for their foray into the garden. The campaign called for subtlety. He had to lead while making it seem as if he were following. So, he did not strike off in the direction of the house. As they approached the place, he sniffed at the air and barked in a way that might have meant any number of things: 'I am hungry' or 'I have seen a small creature' or 'I am one of you and happy to be so.'

Atticus growled. But Frack and Frick had by then sniffed something out for themselves. They headed toward the back of the house, and the others followed. There they found what was indeed a garden. The smell of 'greening' predominated, but it was undercut by enticing counter-currents: cow's flesh, yeast, sugar. The garden was not immediately accessible. It was enclosed by green chain-mesh fencing. There was, however, a door with a latch that Frack easily opened. In no time, the pack was among the lush flowers, vegetables and half-buried goods.

The dogs – all except Benjy – were quietly ecstatic. Along the fence, away from the vegetation, there were pieces of meat and bread. In a far corner, there were chicken breasts and, even, rotting fish! The dogs – all except Benjy – ate their fill. Benjy ate air. He bit at furrows in the ground and made a show of eating, his tail raised and wriggling, until the others had finished. Satisfied, the pack left the garden and made their way back to High Park, wandering about until the sunlight faded and they returned to the coppice.

The first night in their den was so uneventful, Benjy might have said the place they'd discovered had not been a garden of death at all. No one died. All slept soundly and, in fact, returned to the garden the following day and the day after that. (There seemed to be an endless setting of meats, fish and bread.) On the third visit, Benjy's will was tested. Hungry, unconvinced the place was dangerous, he was tempted to eat the meats on the ground. But he ate nothing, choosing instead to bear the pangs a while longer. As they were walking back through the park, scavenging for scavenging's sake, however, Benjy noticed that Frick and Frack were walking in a strange way: wobbling, as if they were about to lose their balance. More than that: the dogs – all save Benjy – had begun to bleed from their muzzles.

That night in the coppice, Benjy was kept awake – and terrified – by the yelps of pain (which he imitated), by the weak thrashing about of his agonizing pack mates (which he aped), by the humid breathing of Frick, Frack and Rosie. When the sun came up, he allowed himself to sniff at the bodies, to take in the death he had brought them. Though Frick, Frack and Rosie were not quite dead, their bodies lay nearly motionless in the coppice. They could neither rise nor communicate. Wary and cautious, Benjy did not abandon them until the following day, when he was certain they were dead.

Atticus, it seemed, had gone off somewhere. Perhaps he had seen death coming and wished to face it on his own. Whatever the case, Benjy never saw the pack leader again. Judging from the agony of the others, however, he was certain the dog was dead.

Of this massacre, Majnoun heard only the sketchiest details. Benjy told it as if some strange sickness or other – one that had spared Benjy himself – had almost completely undone what had once been a strong pack. Just think, said Benjy solemnly: of the dogs who had been in cages on the night of the change, there now remained only two or, perhaps, three alive. Two or three dogs who knew what he and Majnoun knew. For some time, they were quiet.

– I was sorry to see so much death, Benjy said at last.

– Yes, said Majnoun, so much death would make one unhappy.

– Is there water to drink? asked Benjy.

Majnoun was too astute not to notice and mistrust the vagueness in Benjy's account of their pack's final days. But his mistrust was part of the mixed emotions he felt for Benjy. Along with a vague antipathy, there was fraternity. Benjy was the last, or nearly so, of his pack. Majnoun felt a sense of responsibility. As the stronger of the two, he perhaps naturally felt this, but part of him would also have preferred Benjy be elsewhere. He felt apprehensive about something or other, but before deciding what to do with Benjy there was the matter of teaching him human language, as he'd promised.

This proved more difficult than Majnoun had imagined. He himself had begun with a vocabulary of some hundred or so human words. He had then patiently acquired more. He had thought of simply teaching Benjy a vocabulary of essential words and phrases (*food, water, walk, don't touch me, ...*) and then telling him about context and nuance. This was, in fact, how their own original, canine language worked: universally understood *woofs* whose shades of meaning were conveyed by posture, tone or situation. But how was he to teach Benjy that, for humans, certain sounds both did and did not mean what they were supposed to mean? For instance, Majnoun could not imagine a word more fundamental than *food* or the words related to it: *eat, hungry, starving*. He could not easily think of a word about which it was more crucial to be clear. Yet, one evening he and Nira had been in the kitchen together. He had been on the floor, head on his paws, listening as Nira read to him from a newspaper. Miguel came in shirtless from the bedroom and asked

– Are you hungry?

– I could eat, Nira answered.

– What could you eat? asked Miguel.

– What do you have in mind? asked Nira.

– I have sustenance in mind. What did you *think* I had in mind?

– Well, said Nira, if it's only sustenance you want ... I was thinking I had just the food for you, if you don't mind going south.

– I see, said Miguel. In that case, we should retire to consider the menu.

And instead of eating, they had gone to the bedroom, closed the door behind them and, as far as Majnoun could tell from the sounds and odours, they had mated. This had puzzled him for some time. Not because Nira and Miguel had mated, but because they seemed to have conflated two very important things: eating and mating. This struck Majnoun as preposterous. Better if Miguel had come in speaking of some trivial thing (like cleaning the floors) and *that* had meant he wanted to mate. It would have been just as bewildering, but not, somehow, as significant. He began Benjy's lessons in human language with a warning.

– Listen, small dog, he said. Humans do not always mean what is meant by the sounds they make. You must be careful.

– I am sure it is as you say, said Benjy

though Benjy was not at all concerned about the nuances of human language. He wanted only to learn it, seeing how well Majnoun had done for himself. That is, Majnoun's situation was enviable, and Benjy assumed this was down to Majnoun's command of the human tongue.

Benjy was further distracted from the hard truth of Majnoun's warning by the fact that both he and Majnoun had known strange moments with their own language. Prince's way of speaking, for instance:

> We bound into the prairie
> through ages of Winter grass,
> taking the path Ina took.
> Her name long gone,
> though her roads linger.
> The ground will not forget.

or

> Longing to be sprayed (the green snake
> writhing in his master's hand),
> back and forth into that stream –
> jump, rinse: coat slick with soap.

In a word, Benjy was confident that Prince's poetry had prepared him for the complications of human speech.

The months during which Majnoun taught Benjy to speak 'human' (that is, English) were a struggle for all involved. Majnoun taught as any reasonable being might. He made what he knew were significant sounds, so that Benjy could recognize and then produce them for himself. This method was tricky because Majnoun would not speak in Nira's presence. Benjy and Majnoun did their Berlitzing at the far end of the garden, where they could be heard by passersby, though they could not be seen. As sharp as Benjy was – and he was very sharp when driven by self-interest – there were nuances of the language that could not be mastered without interaction with a native speaker. He, like Majnoun himself, tended to mispronounce important words. *Food*, for instance, came out as

– Ooot

while *water* was

– Owta.

The sounds might have been recognizable in context, but acquiring 'context' was difficult. Majnoun did not want him to speak to Nira. In fact, Majnoun had forbidden him from speaking to her. But Benjy was convinced that Nira – who'd taught Majnoun the language – was the one to teach him. So he went around Majnoun, speaking to Nira when Majnoun was asleep or in another room or out relieving himself.

From the beginning, he could pronounce Nira's name well enough that there was never a doubt he was speaking to her. To Nira, it was disconcerting and frightening whenever Benjy, anxious that Majnoun should not know what he was up to, 'whispered' her name.

– Near-a, he'd say

and then he would try a word out. For instance:

– Owta.

– Water? Nira would ask

and Benjy would repeat the word, imitating her and adding

– Pease

which was as close as he ever got to *please*. He would then observe her as she filled the bowl or, more often than not, say

– There's water in the bowl.

At which, Benjy would answer

– Hank ooo

and she would correct him, punctiliousness overcoming the almost unbearable strangeness of being spoken to by a beagle.

Benjy's approach was mildly successful but only until the afternoon he spoke Nira's name and then said, quite clearly

– Mow neigh.

He'd meant to speak the word *money*, a word Majnoun had been unable to explain precisely. The word had something to do with what Majnoun had called 'this for that,' a word that was mysterious and yet palpably important, perhaps the most important. It was also mixed up, somehow, with the thin, round, copper-tangy disks that peppered the streets of the city.

– What? Nira asked.

– Monet, pease.

For a strange moment, Nira was certain the beagle was referring to the French impressionist. The possibility that Benjy knew the history of art was frightening because it was so far beyond belief. But his actual demand was just as intimidating.

– You want money? she asked.

Benjy said

– Yes

and nodded.

– No, said Nira. No, no. I don't have any to give you. Go away.

Not knowing why Nira was upset, Benjy retired from the kitchen, worried that he'd done something wrong. As, indeed, he had. Nira spoke to Majnoun about his 'friend' and, once the dogs were alone, Majnoun attacked Benjy, biting him hard, hurting him until the beagle cried out and went limp in surrender. Majnoun showed himself to be weak, however. He released Benjy without making him bleed. More than that: he warned the dog that worse would happen if he ever spoke to Nira again.

Benjy slunk away with his tail between his legs. In deference to the bigger dog, he did not show himself for a while, hiding behind a couch. He was not afraid of Majnoun. The fact that Majnoun had warned him at all was sufficient proof to Benjy that Majnoun was not dangerous. Majnoun even went on teaching him English! More: in cutting him off from Nira, Majnoun unwittingly forced Benjy to take another (perhaps even better) path to English: Miguel. Miguel was bigger and more threatening than Nira, no doubt more powerful. And an expert speaker of the language. Why should he not speak to Miguel?

There were a few things to consider, of course. How would Miguel respond to his approach? Would he be as upset as Nira? Also, should he tell Majnoun what he was up to? The dog might not be dangerous, but he was overly sensitive and it would be difficult to keep his conversations with Miguel secret from Majnoun.

In the end, Benjy decided to go at it directly. He approached Miguel on an evening when Miguel had finished supper and was alone in the bedroom, reading. Majnoun and Nira were in Nira's room. (Majnoun: eyes closed, legs tucked under him, head resting on the hardwood floor.) Benjy entered the bedroom and sat by the side of the bed until Miguel noticed him. Once he had Miguel's attention, Benjy began with innocent words.

— Want water, he said.

— What? said Miguel. Did you just ask for water?

— Yes, answered Benjy.

Miguel was genuinely pleased.

— You can speak? he asked.

— Little, answered Benjy.

('Ihdle' is how it came out, but it was easily understood.)

— That's fantastic, said Miguel. Did Nira teach you that? Say something else.

As he could not quite catch the sense of 'something else,' Benjy sat still, looking expectantly up at Miguel. Miguel was disappointed.

— She must have taught you more than that, he said. Can you say your name?

— Name Benjy, said Benjy, speaking his own secret name for the first time in his life.

Despite his hesitation in voicing something so private as his secret name — secret because other dogs could not speak it, though it was an intimate sound — his voice was clear, high-pitched and only slightly tremulous.

— Now that's what I'm talking about! said Miguel. Did she teach you any other tricks? Roll over, Benjy. Roll over, boy.

It was puzzling to be asked to 'roll over' after initiating a conversation about water, but these tricks – 'roll over,' 'stand up,' 'play dead,' 'beg,' 'whisper,' 'sing' – were what he did best. They required nothing of him. He held Miguel's gaze a moment and then he rolled over.

As Miguel did not believe the dog could actually speak, he found these tricks more pleasing and more impressive than the dog's request for water. Lifting Benjy into his arms, scratching the fur on the dog's neck and behind its ears, Miguel carried him to Nira's room.

— How did you do this? he asked. It must have taken hours.

— How did I do what?

— How'd you teach the dog to say its name?

— What name?

— Stop pretending like you don't know, said Miguel. Benjy's great. He's a real dog, not like Jim, who lies around the place all day. This one can do things. You should be proud.

— You heard him speak? Nira asked. I didn't teach him. Jim must have.

— Right, said Miguel, because of course Jim can speak.

Miguel was immediately offended by what he took for a coyness on his wife's part. Why shouldn't she tell him how she'd gone about getting Benjy to say his name when asked?

— Fine, said Miguel. I'll teach him something myself.

Which, over the space of a week, he proceeded to do. I'll teach him something unusual, thought Miguel, something more difficult than his name and a handful of words. He decided to teach the dog the first pages of *Vanity Fair*, one of Nira's favourite novels. Thackeray's was the kind of writing that sent English majors everywhere into paroxysms. Though Thackeray's sentences were sometimes long and twisty –

While the present century was in its teens, and on one sunshiny morning in June, there drove up to the great iron gate of Miss Pinkerton's

academy for young ladies, on Chiswick Mall, a large family coach,
with two fat horses in blazing harness, driven by a fat coachman in a
three-cornered hat and wig, at the rate of four miles an hour.

– Miguel found his task remarkably straightforward.

Once Benjy understood that he was meant to repeat (in correct order) the sounds Miguel wished him to repeat, Benjy repeated them. Convinced that the beagle was little more than a good (admittedly unusual) parrot, Miguel was pleased with himself, proud of his heretofore hidden talent as an animal trainer. Every so often, he did find it strange that a beagle should, with increasing finesse, speak of three-cornered hats, fat horses and the iron gates of Miss Pinkerton's academy. But he got used to the strangeness by imagining the look on Nira's face the moment his dog (which is what Benjy quickly became) spoke the first page or so of *Vanity Fair*.

That moment never came, however.

The dynamic in the house had changed. After the 'money' incident, it wasn't so much that Nira disliked Benjy as that she found the dog disingenuous. Whereas she was *un*intimidated by Majnoun's silences, she began to find those moments when Benjy sat up and looked at her disconcerting. It got so she could not work when the beagle was in a room with her. So, Benjy was banished (the door closed against him), made to spend most of the day either alone or alone with Majnoun, until Miguel came home.

Miguel, for his part, began to treat Majnoun with an amused but palpable scorn. He let it be known, now and then, that he was sceptical of Nira's claims for Majnoun's intelligence. His scepticism was usually followed by his asking Benjy to 'roll over' or 'play dead,' as if Benjy's execution of those tricks made his superior intelligence obvious. Of course, Nira would not humiliate Majnoun in that way. She refused to ask Majnoun, for whom she had the greatest respect, to roll around on the carpet in order to prove that he possessed an intelligence she knew very well he *did* possess.

Majnoun, who tolerated Benjy's closeness to Miguel, understood the implications of Miguel's scorn, but he could not understand the scorn itself. For one thing, he would not have guessed that 'intelligence' could be a source of status. It seemed to him that what humans called 'intelligence' (knowing the accepted names for things, performing feats that required a certain mental dexterity) was in every way inferior to the *knowing* he remembered from his previous life as a dog, the life before he was sideswiped by 'thinking.' When it became clear that Miguel gave Benjy higher status because the beagle 'rolled over' and 'played dead,' Majnoun was astounded.

No, he was more and other than astounded. Majnoun understood the implications of Miguel's behaviour better, perhaps, than Miguel did. It was clear that Benjy was angling for status, that he wanted the position Nira had. That thought was intolerable to Majnoun, intolerable on its own but also because it brought back memories of what he'd suffered. And yet, what was he to do? He had warned Benjy. The right thing, now, was to bite the little dog to death. No doubt about it. But could he actually do such a thing? It would mean annihilating a part of himself, taking a final turn away from what had been his life: pack, canidity, coppice.

Benjy, for his part, was pleased at having mastered the skills Miguel admired, and he began to allow Miguel's scorn for Majnoun to influence his own behaviour. For instance, when Majnoun was teaching him language, Benjy would say the word Majnoun wished him to learn, repeat it and then ask to move on to the next word. He knew, now that he was spending time with Miguel, that Majnoun did not have a proper accent, that words as Majnoun said them were not easily understood by humans. In the case of the word *evening*, in fact, Benjy allowed himself to correct Majnoun's pronunciation. He corrected Majnoun respectfully but he corrected him as if he, not Majnoun, were the one who knew human language best. By the time he had memorized – without understanding it – the first page of *Vanity Fair*, Benjy had tentatively begun to practise the geometry of dominance: putting his head (lightly) on Majnoun's back as they lay down together, preceding Majnoun to the food dishes and sniffing at the contents in Majnoun's bowl *before* eating what was in his own, walking before Majnoun whenever he could. Benjy did not realize he was doing this. He was not conscious of it, but Majnoun was.

One afternoon, when Nira had opened the back door for them so they could get a bit of air, Majnoun attacked the smaller dog as ruthlessly as he could. They were in the middle of the yard when Majnoun bit down on the back of Benjy's neck. He'd meant to catch the beagle's throat in his jaws, but at the last moment Benjy had moved his head. Benjy cried out and he knew at once that he had made a mistake: Majnoun was not the dog he'd assumed he was.

There was snow on the ground. It was wet and slippery. The snow saved Benjy's life. Majnoun slipped as he tried to pick the smaller dog up in his jaws – in order to dash the beagle against a cement step. As Majnoun slipped, Benjy wriggled free and cried out

– Nira!

but Majnoun was on him immediately.

There was a gap in the backyard fence, a gap that would (perhaps!) accommodate his body. Benjy ran for it and threw himself in. There was not quite enough space. Much of him went through, but it slowed him down enough that Majnoun managed to bite him again, drawing more blood. Majnoun could not get a proper grip, however. With every muscle in him, Benjy pulled himself through the gap and ran for his life. He did not look back. There was no need. It was clear to both of them that Majnoun wanted only to kill him.

Reason, in so far as it had any place at all, was superfluous.

Some ten minutes after she had opened the door for them, Nira returned to see if the dogs wanted back in. The snow in the yard was, in places, as if frothed up. There were patches of greenish dark earth where the dogs had struggled or stumbled. Not far from where Majnoun stood looking at her, there were also specks of blood on the snow.

– Where's Benjy? Nira asked.

Majnoun shook his head.

– He ran away? she asked.

Majnoun nodded.

– Do you want to come in?

Without answering, Majnoun went in the back door, his wet fur brushing against Nira's pants as he did. She would very much have liked to know that Benjy was all right, but it felt wrong to question Majnoun at that moment. That night, she told Miguel the little she knew of Benjy's disappearance. Over the following weeks it never did feel right to ask Majnoun what had happened. And, in the end, they never spoke of the dog again.

3

ATTICUS'S LAST WISH

Olympus, the city, lies atop Olympus, the mountain. Much more than that cannot be said because it is, as any city is, a correlative of the minds that made it. Travel through Olympus would be a revelation of the imagination that conceived the city. That imagination being divine, no human language can express it. In English – if one must speak English – Olympus is best encompassed by the words *nothing* and *nowhere*, though it is something and somewhere, and he whose mind Olympus best mirrors, Zeus, father of the gods, was unhappy with his sons.

For a number of reasons, Hermes and Apollo had tried to keep their wager secret. The other gods being gods, this was not possible. For one thing, the strangeness of the dogs was immediately obvious to all who cared about such things. The why of their strangeness was unknown, but the who was clear. Hermes spent most of his time on earth and Apollo was fascinated by earthly things. So the brothers were pestered as to their motives. After a while, they grew tired of denying they'd had anything to do with the dogs and admitted that they had wagered on the deaths of the fifteen. In so doing, they sowed a kind of frenzy among the gods, all of whom immediately made wagers of their own.

When Zeus discovered what his sons had done, he sent for them.

– How could you have been so cruel? he asked.

– Why cruel? asked Apollo. Mortals suffer. What have we done to make their suffering worse?

– He's right, Father, said Hermes. Wipe them out if you don't want them to suffer.

– They suffer within their own bounds, said Zeus. These poor dogs don't have the same capacities as humans. They weren't made to bear doubt or to know that their deaths will come. With their senses and instincts, they'll suffer twice as much as humans do.

– You're not suggesting humans are brutes, are you? asked Apollo.

Hermes laughed.

– The only thing certain about humans *is* their brutishness, he said.

– You two are worse than humans, said Zeus.

– There's no need to insult us, said Apollo.

– Be grateful I'm not going to punish you. The damage has been done. But I don't want you interfering with these creatures anymore. You've done enough. Leave them whatever peace they can find.

From that moment, all the gods knew Zeus's will and, for the most part, abided by his edict. They did not interfere with the dogs. Interference, when it came, came from an unexpected quarter: Zeus himself. Taking pity on his favourite, Atticus, the father of the gods intervened in the life of the dogs.

Contrary to Benjy's impressions, Atticus was thoughtful, sensitive and, to an extent, altruistic. He was a committed leader, capable of – or prone to – instinctive decisions. More: he could put aside thought in the service of forceful action. But in quiet moments his sensitivity sometimes led him to reconsider his own behaviour. In other words, Atticus had a conscience, and it was this that led him to what some would call faith.

Not long after the night in the veterinary clinic, Atticus came to believe that the canine was dying in him, that this was a tragedy, that the loss of the old ways would prove disastrous. This naturally led him to consider what it was that made him a dog. Was it his senses? Perhaps. But then he still had his senses. Was it something physical? Yes, it was in the way he felt as he ran, as he drank water, as he dug the ground with his claws. But his physical self, too, was unchanged. In fact, as he catalogued the things that made him a dog, Atticus changed his mind. The canine was not dying in him or in the eleven with him. Rather, it was being obscured by the new thinking, the new perspectives, the new words. These needed to be pushed aside, like curtains before a necessary vantage.

In the early days, Atticus had had his vivid memories of the previous life to guide him. In those days, memories of the previous life were a lure to them all. Some were, naturally, more devoted to the life that had been. It had been easy to discover who was willing to fight alongside him for a return to old ways: no strange language, no twisting thoughts, the senses alive. Once the pack had rid itself of threats to this ideal – once they had killed or chased off Majnoun, Athena, Bella, Prince and Bobbie – Atticus was satisfied that they could live as dogs ought to live. In the aftermath of the cleansing, the pack followed Atticus's precepts:

1. No strange talk. This above all because, to his dying day, Atticus disliked what he remembered of the dog who disappeared:

> In the sunny world, with its small
> things moving too fast,
> I shy away from light
> and in the attic cuss the dark.

2. A strong leader (that is, Atticus himself)
3. A good den
4. The weak in their proper place

Of the killings, only one troubled Atticus's conscience: the killing of the Duck Toller, Bobbie. He, the twins and Max had been so filled with fervour for the old life that they had behaved in a way that was not in keeping with the canine. They had killed the Duck Toller in a frenzy of which he was, in retrospect, ashamed. Worse: the death of the smaller dog was a signal that he – that *they* – had overlooked something important: the sanctity of the echelon. This became clear when the two smaller dogs fled.

On the morning that Benjy and Dougie went missing, Atticus had a presentiment of the problems the pack would face. With a kind of symmetry, Atticus and Benjy – the top and the bottom dog – came to the same thought from different ends of the spectrum: the weak were, after all, of more than passing importance. Something was 'off' without the two on the lower rung. There was now an emptiness at the bottom, so to speak. They were, unexpectedly, in need of weakness. Atticus was the biggest and strongest of the dogs that remained. Frick and Frack, together, might have had a chance against him, but the brothers would suffer if they challenged him, and all of them knew it. On the other hand, it would have been unthinkable to use either Frick or Frack as low dog. The brothers were unnaturally close and neither would have accepted a diminished position. That left Rosie and Max.

If they had truly become dogs again, Rosie would have been the obvious candidate. She was not necessarily the weakest of them, but she was female. And this was, to the males, a mark against her. But Rosie had become important to Atticus, the smell of her something he wanted for himself alone. His own feelings confused and humiliated him. Rosie was not in heat. It wasn't that he wanted to fuck her. It was something unnameable and unfamiliar, a perversion for which the dogs had no name.

(Though Atticus had a developed sense of transgression, he did not have a notion of 'sin.' If he had, he might have accepted that his feelings for Rosie were – by his own thinking – sinful. They were transgressions against the canine. And yet, how comforting. At times, he and Rosie sat together by Wendigo Pond, away from the others, and used the forbidden language. Had they been caught, Atticus would have insisted they were innocent, that his conversations with Rosie were not, as they had been with Majnoun, deeply reasoned. She was something like a confidante or a lieutenant. Nothing more. So he might have said, but in his heart Atticus knew that his feelings were not innocent. They were sexual and they were unclear.)

So Max became low dog.

Except that Max was not co-operative. The dog felt he deserved status, having helped the pack rid itself of undesirables. Atticus understood Max's unhappiness, but the pack had changed and Max would have to change with it or suffer the consequences.

Except that Max made them *all* suffer the consequences. He would not allow himself to be mounted. He had to be attacked, threatened, bitten. Frick and Frack would work in tandem, one holding Max by the neck while the other mounted him. Atticus had an easier time of it. He was pack leader, and Max, though resentful, accepted that it was Atticus's right to mount him whenever he liked. The real problem was Rosie. The German shepherd was just strong enough to impose her will, but Max fought her because he could not stand to be mounted by one he was convinced he could overcome.

Because it sometimes took too long for Rosie to mount Max, Atticus would growl and threaten, nipping at Max's ears to get the dog to submit. This was not the way true dogs did things, though, and they all knew it. Max had every right to contest his status. Why should Atticus intervene? In the end, the disappearance of the smaller dogs was a disaster for all of them. Their mornings began warily and their evenings ended on the same wary note.

It was during this time that Atticus began to pray.

He already had a notion of what an ideal or pure dog might be: a creature without the flaws of thought. As time went on, he attributed to this pure being all the qualities he believed to be noble: sharp senses, absolute authority, unparalleled prowess at hunting, irresistible strength. Somewhere, thought Atticus, there must be a dog like this. Why? Because one of the qualities his ideal canine possessed was *being*. An 'ideal' dog that did not exist could not be truly ideal. Therefore, the dog of dogs, as Atticus conceived it, *had* to exist. It had to *be*. (Atticus imagined this dog existing without red; that is, without the colour the dogs had gained with their change in thinking.) More: if Atticus's pure dog existed – as it must – why should it not feel his longing for guidance? Why should it not find him?

Atticus followed his feelings. He humbled himself before his pure dog. He found a place away from the den. It was on the other side of Grenadier Pond, among the tall grass and trees. He cleared the ground of leaves and, every evening, he brought a portion of the things he had caught or scavenged. Every evening at the same time: mice, pieces of bread, bits of hot dog, rats, birds, whatever he had saved from his share of the pack's food. And, speaking the forbidden language, every evening he asked for guidance from the one leader he was prepared to follow.

The gods are compelled by rhythm – as is the universe, as are all the creatures in it. And so, Atticus's regular prayers and repeated ritual at length caught Zeus's attention. The father of the gods heard the dog's wishes and was moved by its sacrifices and faith. Appearing to Atticus in a dream, Zeus took the form of a Neapolitan mastiff: his coat rumpled as the skin of an elephant, his jowls a grey cascade. And Zeus spoke to Atticus in the new language of the pack.

– Atticus, said the god, I am the one to whom you sacrifice.

– I knew you would come, said Atticus. Tell me how I may be a better dog.

– You are no longer a dog, said Zeus. You are changed. But you are mine and I pity you your fate. I cannot intervene in your life. I have myself forbidden it. But I will grant you a wish at your death. Whatever you wish for at the moment before your spirit ascends, I will grant.

– But, Great Dog, what good is a wish if I must die for it?

– I can do no more, said Zeus.

And at these words, the father of the gods turned to ash in Atticus's dream and drifted above a bright green field where a thousand small, dark creatures ran.

In the months that followed, Atticus maintained his shrine and continued to speak to Zeus, comforted that the Great Dog had heard his pleas, grateful for what he imagined to be the god's attention. His prayers did not prevent the tragedies that beset the pack, however. First, Frick and Frack wounded Max and he (Atticus) was forced to finish the dog off. Then, Frick, Frack and he himself killed the small dog (Dougie) on his return. An accident: the bigger dogs were fired by blood lust, angry for the trouble the dog's departure had caused. (Atticus asked Zeus's forgiveness for this transgression, but, really, it was something of a miracle that they had not killed Benjy as well. In the grip of what felt like instinct but was only anger, they might have killed any number of dogs. The lesson, painfully acquired with Bobbie, then learned again at Dougie's death: violence has reasons that reason itself cannot know.) Finally, there came the poisoning.

On the pack's first foray into the garden of death, Atticus followed Frick and Frack into the garden, convinced the ground's bounty was a gift from the one who'd come to him in a dream. His first premonition of death came while he was eating a piece of chicken: flesh that tasted as certain dog toys smell. It was not the way anything should taste, but it also tasted of chicken and it was good. Shortly thereafter, death stepped out from behind its curtain. Atticus's nose began to bleed. He could not drink enough water. His insides burned. He had eaten more than the others. His symptoms were the first to appear.

It was after his second feast in the garden of death that Atticus knew for certain something was not right. Though he couldn't tell *how* his pack had been done, he knew it had been. Some thing or some being had got to them. And he, their leader, had done nothing. So, while the others made their way back to the coppice to die, Atticus went to his shrine. By then, thirst was like a fire that ravaged the kindling of his bones and sinews. Death was on him and he knew it.

With his last words, Atticus asked that the one responsible for his pack's demise be punished. Then, the dog died, ever-faithful, filled with the hope that his unseen enemy would suffer at the hands of his god.

Having escaped Majnoun's anger, Benjy did not know where to go or what to do. He had imagined himself living with Miguel, Nira and Majnoun, staying and mastering human language. Though he knew otherwise, he convinced himself that Majnoun had overreacted, that his (that is, Benjy's) manoeuvring – his courting of Miguel's favour, for instance – had been innocent or, at worst, experimental. As far as Benjy was concerned, he hadn't given Majnoun cause to bite him. Majnoun would come to his senses and allow him back. He was certain of it, but, in the meantime, where would he stay?

It was spring, the third week in April. There was still snow on the ground, especially in tree-shaded yards and in High Park. It was not the worst time to find oneself outdoors. During the day, the streets were dry and warm. Benjy, of course, knew the area around the park well. If he stayed in Parkdale or High Park, there would be dogs to be avoided but he could usually spot those quickly, so he was not afraid. (The white dogs with black spots were the worst. It wasn't so much their aggression; other dogs were sometimes even more aggressive. It was that they were – without question – the stupidest creatures on earth, and that was even if one included cats. It was useless to try reasoning with them, whatever language one chose. Worse, you could never tell when one of them would come at you. It was not in his nature to hate other dogs, but Benjy disliked Dalmatians the way some humans dislike men named Steve or Biff.)

He was at the corner of Fern and Roncesvalles, trying to decide where he should go, when a ruddy-faced old man bent down and scooped him into his arms, saying

– Who's a pretty doggy? Who's a pretty boy?

This was most unpleasant. Benjy squirmed as if he were helplessly sinking into a pond of foul-smelling wool. From out of a pocket in his overcoat, the man extracted a biscuit that smelled of sugar, fish, carrots, lamb and rice. Suspicious, but captivated by the smell of the biscuit, Benjy stopped wriggling. He sniffed at the biscuit again, taking in the hints of salt, canola oil, rosemary, human sweat and apple.

– What is it? Benjy asked, speaking English.

As if it were natural for dogs to address him, the old man said:

– It is a biscuit. I was told dogs like them. Do you not want it?

Sniffing again at the air close to the biscuit, Benjy decided that the thing was what the man said it was: food. He took the biscuit from the man's hand and, crunching it with the teeth on one side of his mouth, he allowed himself to eat what was, in the end, a memorable treat.

– Thank you, said Benjy.

The man put him down and absent-mindedly rubbed the fur along his back.

– You're welcome, he said. I'm glad you liked it. I've got to go, now, Benjy. See you later.

It was a moment before Benjy realized the man had used his secret name. Did the human know him, then? He looked in the direction the man had gone and, almost instinctively, followed him. This was not as easy as it should have been. In Benjy's experience, the humans that smelled as the old man had – that is, of wool, sugary urine, sweat and some indefinable decay – were slower than others. Not this one. He walked quickly. Then, too, it was a busy day along Roncesvalles. There were any number of obstructions: women with baby strollers, other dogs, and – worst of all – ambling humans who were always a threat to step on you or kick you out of the way. Then there were the distractions: post boxes, lampposts, garbage bins, telephone poles, the sour milk and roast chicken smell of the Sobey's, the raspberry jam from a bakery, the sausage and cheese from the delis along the street ... so many things that made you want to stop and smell them. Keeping up with the man was a task. Yet, Benjy did keep up, the grey of the man's pants – the colour of ash – always before him.

The old man – Zeus in mortal guise – walked south to the end of Roncesvalles, crossed the street on a diagonal and stepped onto the waiting streetcar. Abandoning caution, Benjy followed and jumped onto the streetcar just as its doors were closing. He easily found the old man – who was sitting at the back – and stood up to put his paws on the man's leg. As if it were unexceptional to be importuned by a dog, the old man helped Benjy up onto the window seat.

Benjy's feelings were mixed. He was not used to streetcars and he found their motion and noise disconcerting. (He had last been on a streetcar years previously, with his mistress, and he had not at all enjoyed the ride.) But then, there was the old man beside him: a peculiar presence but kindly, and if there was one thing Benjy knew, it was that kindness could be exploited. In the end, though, the thing that settled him down – or distracted him from his disquiet – was the window. It was open just enough for him to stick his snout through and take in the scented districts of Queen Street: from the musty oleo of Parkdale, past a bridge that smelled as if it were made of pigeon shit, past grasses and urine-saturated posts, past boutiques that exhaled dust or perfume or the smell of new cloth, back to old neighbourhoods, sumac trees and maples; the fishy-mineral lake a constant, intoxicating emanation. It was all intoxicating; so much so that Benjy was in Leslieville before he knew it and before he realized that the old man was no longer beside him, had disappeared god knows when.

Though the streetcar was not full, someone must have complained about Benjy, because at Woodbine, just past a place that smelled of human shit (in all its lovely complexity, but adulterated by something that reminded him of a garden of death), the streetcar's driver strode toward him.

– Whose dog is this? the man asked the air.

You could tell he was not friendly.

Benjy jumped down from the seat before the driver could grab him. He scampered to the front of the streetcar and, the doors being open, tumbled down the steep steps and into what was, in effect, a new country: unknown, a little frightening. Walking past a gas station, he went south, instinctively heading toward the lake.

It wasn't long before he was on the beach. The trees were still skeletal, their just-budding leaves like lime-green nubs. This time of year especially, a dog couldn't help himself: one just needed to bite something. It was as if one's teeth had desires of their own. So, snapping up a supple and tough twig, Benjy set off along the shore with no destination in mind, the sand stiff and cold beneath his paws.

Of the fifteen who'd been changed by Apollo, Benjy was the dog who had best made peace with the new way of thinking. Essentially selfish, he used his intelligence almost uniquely to serve his own wants, needs, desires and whims. He was not often troubled by pointless speculation. Yet, there were moments when, in a manner of speaking, his intelligence took on a mind of its own. Now, for instance, looking out at the great expanse of water, Benjy wondered why it was there. Why should this bluish, non-land be? And how far did it extend?

These thoughts reminded him, briefly, of the dog who had disappeared:

> The leaves, they run like mice,
> while birds peck at the ground.
> The wood has rotted in its bin.
> The grim axe has come round

But Benjy's mind was soon on to other, more important things. What would he eat and where would he stay for the night? If the humans here (beside this stretch of the endless water) were at all like those near High Park, he would surely find one to take care of him. Biting down on the tough stick, he continued along the beach, heading east.

Happy, Benjy was too distracted to notice a mutt who cautiously approached. By the time he saw the dog – and was almost overcome by panic, because he could not immediately read the dog's intent – the mutt was all over him, jumping up and down, sniffing at his anus and genitals, barking like one about to die of pleasure.

— You are the small dog from my pack! said the mutt, tail wagging madly.

At those words, spoken in a language only one of the fifteen could have understood, Benjy recognized the dog who had disappeared. That is, Prince. (How unpredictable life is, thought Benjy. I was just thinking about this dog.)

— Dog who was gone, where have you been? Benjy asked.

— He remembers! cried Prince. You remember our way of speaking!

His joy surpassing his capacity to express it with words, Prince began to run in wide circles around the beagle, tongue lolling out. It was as if he were chasing the delight that animated him. Benjy knew what Prince's running meant, of course, but he did not share the feeling. He had lived through strange times with Majnoun and, before that, with the pack he had killed off. That Prince was a member of that nearly extinct group did not make Benjy glad.

— Dog, he said, stop running.

— I have been in exile for so long, cried Prince, I thought I'd lost our language.

— Our language isn't important, said Benjy. The human language is what matters.

— The human language? asked Prince. It is all noise. Do you speak it?

— I do, said Benjy. I will teach you what I know, if you like.

— Perhaps a few words, if you like, said Prince without enthusiasm.

Benjy walked toward the lake, taking in the tang of it. What did it matter, he thought, if the dog clung to his ignorance.

— Where have you been? Benjy asked.

Prince had been many places since they'd last seen each other, but none of the places he'd been was as significant to him as the place he'd fled (High Park, the coppice) or the pack from which he'd been driven.

— What has happened to the other dogs? Prince asked.

With little emotion, Benjy gave him a severely truncated version of events. The others were all dead, he said, all poisoned by some unknown hand. And he himself had barely escaped with his life. In this way – brutally, with no mention of Majnoun – Prince learned of his pack's devastation.

O, what it was to be swept so suddenly through such a range of feelings! From joy to despair in a matter of moments. Prince sat up and keened. And his cries were such an unfettered expression of grief that even the humans in the distance stopped to listen.

– We are the last, said Prince.

– Yes, said Benjy. It is all very sad. But tell me what has happened to you.

Benjy was not curious about Prince's fate. What he wanted to know was whether or not Prince had learned anything useful. Prince, garrulous by nature, answered Benjy as best he could. But having just been devastated by the knowledge that he'd lost almost all of those who spoke his language, his heart was not in it.

After following Hermes out of the coppice, Prince began what was, unbeknownst to him, a long trek east. He hadn't wanted to abandon his pack or lose the thing that mattered so much to him: the new language. He thought to remain in the park, avoiding the others until time had passed and their rage had quelled, but it was as if an undercurrent drew him farther and farther from the den.

To begin with, that winter, he was adopted by a family in Parkdale. He was happy, but when the spring came he lost them as he chased after a squirrel in a neighbourhood he did not know. The loss was not painful. He did not look for the family again. For a time, he was fed by a human whose breath and ear canals smelled of rancid fish. The rancid human lived east of Parkdale. Farther east still, in Trinity-Bellwoods, he was attacked by a German shepherd and then taken in by a sympathetic human who fed him until his wounds healed. She had smelled of a breeze coming in off the prairie and he would have stayed with her, but, after a time, she stopped letting him in.

From there – south of Dundas and Manning – he was abducted. That is, he was lured into a vehicle driven by adults but filled with young humans. He ended up somewhere far north of the lake: off Avenue Road, south of Eglinton. Prince was, fundamentally, good-natured. He was curious about the world and all that was in it, but here the younger humans would not let him alone. There was always some child – breath smelling of sugar and summer berries – draped around his neck like a kerchief of monkey. Despite this, he would have stayed on. In most ways, the humans were kind. The one way in which they were not, however, was in the leash they chose for him. It was a choke chain that he could not look at without feeling trepidation.

Most of the leash was black leather. The leather had a clip that fastened onto a metal ring. The metal ring was attached to a silver chain made of metal links that was itself fastened to a metal ring. Once around his neck, the silver chain either hung loosely or, when pulled, constricted and strangled him. This was not only unpleasant in itself, but, when he was occasionally attacked by other dogs, he had to choose between strangulation (as the human tried to hold him back) or defence. That is, he was either bitten or choked. This turned walking with the humans into a daily source of anxiety. And so, feeling that he would go strange if he stayed, Prince opened the front door for himself one night and wandered off.

After Avenue and St. Clair, he again drifted east, going from this plate of food to that treat, staying sometimes in people's yards, scavenging for food in back alleys and behind restaurants. Moving across the city while sniffing out the lake, which was, when the wind was right, like a tantalizing hint of mineral and algae, a hint quickly lost in the congeries of city smells.

Having moved across Toronto in a rough parabola (from High Park not far from the lake north to Eglinton then south and east to the Beach below Victoria Park and Queen), Prince would have been hard-pressed to say *what* the city was. Not its dimensions – which did not interest him – but its essence. Certainly, it had a particular heft in the mind. It was different from Ralston, where he'd been whelped and where his first and still-beloved master had lived. Ralston was 'home.' It was an ache within him and always would be.

Toronto was, above all, a place for humans, their warm dens and unpredictable moods. It reeked of them: from the pleasing musk of their genitals and arses to the sweet, compound fragrances that clung to them. They were the city's hazard and its sanctuary, its sense and its point. But what Prince loved about the city, the reason it was the setting for most of his poems, was the way it smelled. Whatever else he might be feeling or thinking, there was always some distracting smell to consider: humans, of course, but so much more, from the rotting carcasses of small animals around Grenadier Pond to the mouth-watering emanations from curry houses around Danforth and Victoria Park. A dog would have to be dead not to appreciate the sheer variety of the city's reeks.

At this point, bored by Prince's account of his travels, Benjy said

– Yes, yes, but where do you sleep and what do you eat?

– I do not sleep in any one place, said Prince. I know of a number of dens where the humans feed me and let me stay inside.

– Are these dens nearby? asked Benjy. I am hungry.

– One is near, said Prince. Shall I take you?

– Will the humans feed me?

Prince thought about it for a moment. He'd never brought another dog with him to any of the places he knew, but then he had never encountered one of his pack mates out here by the lake. *One* of his pack mates? The last one and, so, the most important, worth more to him than all the humans together.

– I do not know why they would not feed you, he said.

And he led Benjy on a longish trek to a house near Rhodes and Gerrard.

The house in question was small and rickety, looking a little like it might tip over. It was white (or whitish), its porch trimmed in a grandmotherly blue. Though it was late afternoon, Prince said

– They are not awake this early. We will have to wait.

Which they did, lying side by side on the porch. As they waited, Prince recounted more of his time away from the pack, his impressions of the city, interrupting his narrative to speak one of his newer poems:

With one paw, trying
the edges of the winter pond,
finding its waters solid,
he advances, nails sliding,
still far from home.

While listening to Prince, Benjy experienced a feeling he rarely felt: boredom. He knew no word for boredom, but the feeling was accompanied by a nearly palpable desire to have Prince stop talking. It was not that Prince was in the least offensive. It was that nothing the dog said was of use to Benjy. Besides, he hated the trouble it took to understand some of the words. He felt relief when the screen door screeched and a human stepped onto the porch. It was a man, tall and imposing, his hair black.

He lit a cigarette and then, seeing the dogs, he called out:

– Clare! Your dog brought a friend!

Then dimly, from inside the house:

– What?

– Your dog! It brought another dog with it!

The screen door screeched again and out stepped a short woman in a pink terrycloth robe: hair as dark as the man's, eyes outlined in kohl. She took a drag on the man's cigarette, then reached down to pat Prince's back.

– Hi, Russell, she said. Hi, boy! Where you been?

Prince flinched at her touch, a ripple travelling along his flanks.

– You see that? said the man. He's got fleas.

– He doesn't have fleas! Leave him alone!

Having so recently observed a human couple 'up close' and having spent time learning the rudiments of their language, Benjy assumed he understood the dynamic between the humans before him. More: he saw an opportunity to make a place for himself. So, when the female had finished asserting that Prince had no fleas, Benjy suddenly got up on his hind legs, put his front paws together as if he were praying and recited the beginning of *Vanity Fair*:

— Eye'll tuh pro-sent sendry wass een eets teens an un-shy-nee ore-ning een June …

That was as far as Benjy got before he blanked, but he had made an impression. Though they had trouble with the dog's accent, the couple recognized the rhythms of speech. They looked at Benjy in wonder, as if he were an impossibility. A good ten seconds passed before the man said

— What in the fuck was that?

— I don't know, said Clare. Is he talking?

Suddenly and with unexpected grace, the man picked Benjy up by the scruff of the neck and, with Benjy's snout near his own nose, asked

— Do you talk?

Benjy could, of course, in his limited way, talk. What he could not do was speak while his neck was learning the weight of his arse. He struggled in the man's grip, increasingly uncomfortable, managing only a kind of half-bark, half-plea.

— Put him down, said Clare. How's he going to talk if you're strangling him?

— This is how dogs are *supposed* to be picked up, said the man.

But he put Benjy down.

Prince, who'd jumped off the porch, called to his pack mate.

— Let's go, he said. The big human is not always good.

But Benjy sat at the man's feet, tail wagging expectantly.

— You see? said the man. I didn't hurt him.

— Yeah, but you scared Russell, said Clare.

— Who cares? asked the man. I bet *this* one does tricks.

To Benjy, he said

— Roll over!

Which Benjy did.

— Play dead! the man said.

Which Benjy did.

— Dance!

Which Benjy did, getting up on his hind legs and turning in neat circles.

– Talk! said the man.

And once again, Benjy recited as much as he remembered of *Vanity Fair.*

– The little fucker's gold, said the man.

Though she had affection for 'her' dog, Clare agreed. It was almost as if the beagle understood them. Beyond that, the dog was compact and adorable. Much of her affection for Russell was transferred to Benjy on the spot.

– He must belong to someone, she said.

– No, said Benjy. No, no, no!

– You heard him, the man said laughing. He doesn't belong to anyone. Besides, possession is nine-tenths of the law.

– You think we should keep him?

– Don't see why not. He hasn't got tags. What's your name, boy? Can you say your name?

– Benjy, said Benjy.

– Henny? asked Clare.

– Benjy, said Benjy again.

– Benny it is, said the man.

He opened the screen door to let Benjy into the house. Prince climbed tentatively onto the porch, intending to follow his pack mate in.

– No, not you, said the man.

He stuck his foot out to block Prince's way. Nor did Clare object. She yawned and went in after Benjy, closely followed by the man, who closed both doors after him. In this way, as suddenly as he'd regained a pack mate, Prince lost the dog he believed was the last to share his language. Over the months that followed, he returned regularly to the house. On occasion, he was chased away. On occasion, he sat on the porch waiting to be let in, hoping to speak with Benjy. As it happened, however, this was the last he saw of the small dog with floppy ears.

The man's name was Randy. This Benjy learned quickly because Randy taught him to say it. And the man was delighted when, in mere hours, Benjy mastered the *r.*

Randy would say

– Hey! Clare! Look what I taught him ...

Then Benjy would speak the name, rolling the *r* as if beagles were French.

– Rrr-andy.

The humans would laugh, and Benjy – who had no idea why the name provoked such pleasure – would look at them with his head tilted to one side. Something in the sound of the name must have been potent because, later, when Randy grew tired of the game, he would ask not

– What's my name?

but

– How do you feel?

The answer

– Rrr-andy

would set the humans laughing as obstreperously as before.

They were, Benjy thought, strange, and over the months he spent with them, he got to observe the strangeness up close. But there were also ways in which they were unexceptional. When they wanted food, they ate. When they were thirsty, they drank. Their den, naturally, was arranged to satisfy these needs at once. When they were in the kitchen, they were never more than a step or two from food or drink. The fridge was – as all fridges are – remarkable in that respect. This one was a wide, tall block of celadon: unavoidable or, better, unmissable. Once its door was opened, it exhaled fat, sweet and spices. Other nooks were just as enticing. The high cupboards, for instance, seemed to be made of coconut, sugar, flour, salt and vinegar. And then there was the room where the humans bathed and applied chemicals to themselves. The bathroom was fascinating, it being astonishing to watch the already pale beings applying creams to make themselves paler still. Was there something about white that brought status? If so, what was the point of drawing black circles around their eyes or red ones around their mouths?

But if the bathroom was astonishing and the kitchen admirable, what was the word for the bedroom? Here, the two were at their strangest. The bedroom had its pleasures, of course. It was where the three of them – Benjy, Randy, Clare – slept. It was where they were a pack, where Benjy felt most as if he belonged. In the beginning, he was relegated to the foot of the bed, but after a while, he slept closer to the middle, ending up most mornings comfortably lodged between the humans. And so, the bedroom was also the room where the smells human bodies made were most pungent.

What was strange about the bedroom was neither the room nor the sensual *there*-ness of its human occupants. What was strange was copulation. The humans had – every now and again – what was called 'sex.' (Why they needed a name for something so obvious was beyond Benjy's understanding. Why name it, when its necessity was clear to all concerned?) The coupling was not confusing. The ritual that accompanied coupling was what Benjy found odd.

First of all, Randy and Clare kicked him off the bed whenever they were about to have sex. If he got anywhere near them when they were aroused, one or the other would treat him as unkindly as they could: kick, slap or hit. While they had sex, he was not wanted, so he kept his distance, observing them from a corner of the room. He would jump onto the wicker chair beside the chest of drawers. From there, he got the best view.

In the real world, in the world of kitchens, bathrooms, televisions and biscuits, Randy was so obviously the leader that it made no sense to respect Clare. Benjy would lie on her lap while she watched television, lick her face to catch any scraps of food that might linger there, put his head above hers when she was lying down. With Randy he was cautious and much more attentive. Randy was like most high-status beings: he hit out when he was displeased. (The only time Benjy tried to jump up on his lap, Randy pushed him away so hard Benjy flew against a table leg.) He was, at least to Benjy, intimidating.

In the bedroom, however, things were not so clear-cut. Most of the time, Randy fucked Clare. There was nothing unusual about that.

It was his prerogative and, really, Benjy would not have been offended if Randy had fucked him as well. But then there were those sessions that smelled of cow. During these, Randy would wear black leather (with parts of himself exposed) and plead while Clare struck him with a riding crop. Most remarkably, it was then *she* who would penetrate Randy. More: Randy's pleadings were, in the bedroom, as pathetic as Clare's sometimes were in the real world, yet both of them seemed to desire these moments during which Clare was fully and admirably dominant while Randy was, to Benjy's thinking, contemptible.

Benjy, a student of dominance, naturally understood that pleasure – the pleasure taken by Randy and Clare in these sessions – changed the equation between beings. As Randy actually enjoyed the moments when he was dominated, it could not mean that he had ceased to be pack leader. Nor could Clare's pleasure in the bedroom give proof that her status had changed elsewhere, that he (that is, Benjy) should now respect her. Yet, something about seeing Randy vulnerable could not help but influence Benjy's feelings about the man. He began to think less of Randy from the first time he saw him in leather and thought progressively less of him on each occasion thereafter.

In effect, Randy and Clare's love life created a kind of vacuum in Benjy's imagination. He could not decide who was actually pack leader. That being the case, he wondered why the leader should not be him. So, after a while, he would not come when Randy called, would not repeat Randy's name, would not immediately submit to Randy's will, running beneath the bed or sofa rather than doing what he was asked to do, peeing on Randy's pillow to let Randy know who was in charge. The result? Randy – not a particularly sensitive man nor one with a deep love for animals – grew tired of Benjy, despite the beagle's intelligence, despite Benjy's obvious talents.

Clare's affection was more durable, but only just. Once Benjy ceased doing what he was told to do (dance, roll over, speak . . .), it occurred to her that they had overestimated his abilities, that the dog was less intelligent than 'Russell,' her dog, the one Randy had chased away and now would not let in. Clare took care of Benjy, though, buying him food and petting him when he allowed it.

Naturally, this all contributed to Benjy's feeling that he was in control.

In total, Benjy spent six months with Randy and Clare, neither a long time nor a short one.

In the weeks immediately preceding his death, his life was just this side of perfect. He had the run of a house. Clare worked during the day on most days. Randy stayed at home but spent much of his time in the living room before the television, out of Benjy's way. When he remembered Benjy or if Benjy prompted him, he would put food down in a bowl – human food, mostly – or let him out the front door so Benjy could relieve himself on the lawn. Otherwise, Benjy was left to his own devices. This was more than a dog of his size and stature could have hoped for: food, a den with humans he could manipulate or evade, and an outside world that was not threatening. If it is possible to grow feral through an excess of civilization, then Benjy grew feral. Ignoring his instincts, abandoning his natural caution, confusing self-indulgence for dominance, losing himself in the twists and turns of his own calculations, he lost sight of the true indicators of dominance.

Randy and Clare should not have been a puzzle to Benjy. They were not complex. What they were was inconsiderate, crooked and above all selfish. In a word, they were very like Benjy himself. When, five months after taking Benjy in, Clare lost her job, the two were three months in arrears on their rent. Randy refused to work at anything that did not involve his 'profession.' (He thought of himself as a musician, though he was actually, from time to time, a roadie. In fact, he did not like music and, being almost proudly shiftless, he had been fired by every band he had ever managed to work for.) Clare, peeved, refused to look for work until he did. Their impasse was unpleasant and tense, but the two agreed on one thing: they would abandon the house rather than pay the rent they owed. In the middle of an October night, taking only what they wanted – and what would fit in their Pontiac Sunbird – they would leave Toronto for Syracuse, where Randy's brother lived.

And so, Benjy's death began *sotto voce.* The trees had changed colour. Along Rhodes, the leaves on the branches that hung over the street were orange and yellow. Nothing unusual about that. Clare was home during the day, but that was no threat to Benjy's routine, so he thought nothing of it. Randy and Clare began to put things in cardboard boxes, but the things they packed held no significance for Benjy, so he was unimpressed. A tension crept into Randy's and Clare's voices. Benjy noticed the change in their demeanour, but as he now thought himself pack leader, it would have been beneath him to acknowledge the shift.

To their credit, on the night they stole away, Randy and Clare tried to take Benjy with them. They had quietly loaded the Sunbird with pots, pans, clothes and lamps. Around one in the morning, when they were ready to leave, they tried to coax Benjy out from under the bed. He refused to follow them. Clare pled their case, but Benjy did not respect Clare. In fact, he was deaf to any counsel but his own.

– Leave the little twerp right there, said Randy. We've got to go.

– We can't leave Benny. He'll starve.

– No, he won't. Menzies'll find him. Besides, I'm tired of his pissing on the pillows.

Clare sighed.

– Stupid dog, she said.

They left the light on in the kitchen. They put down a bowl of water and a bowl of pasta and tuna for the dog. Then they left for their new lives. Clare wept as they walked away from what had been, for five whole years, their home.

The sound of Clare's crying troubled Benjy's dreams. He felt something of her emotion and, roused from sleep, he lifted his head and breathed in. All smelled as it should have and the house was quiet, so he settled back into a dream of quick rats.

The following day, Benjy woke early. Sometime in the night, he had climbed onto the bed. Had he noticed the humans were not there with him? He certainly noticed in the morning. He was alone at the head of a bed without sheets, the light of an autumn morning coming through the now uncurtained bedroom window. He jumped down and cautiously explored the house, the only sounds being the loud hum of the fridge, the clicking of his nails on wood (bedroom, living room, dining room), linoleum (kitchen), ceramic tile (bathroom). There were also the sounds from outside: cars, mostly, and distant voices.

For the first time in a while, Benjy called out Randy's name.

– Rrr-andy!

The sound did not quite echo, but it held in the air a little longer than usual. It was as if words persisted when there were no humans around to hear them. He was not upset. Randy and Clare had not got his permission to leave. They would return. He ate a few bites of pasta and tuna, drank from his water bowl, then returned to the bed. He peed in the place on the bed where Randy's pillow should have been before going back to sleep.

That was, more or less, how the first days passed. Benjy slept, padded about, drank from his bowl (and then the toilet), waited. The days were measured by the slowed passage of time, by darkness and by light. But as time passed, he grew more and more hungry. The first morning, Benjy had been less than thrilled to find pasta and tuna in his bowl. He'd nevertheless eaten every bit by the end of the day. By the end of the second day, he had licked the bowl so clean there was no hint of tuna left on the porcelain. From that moment, the house became a place in which to search for food.

The fridge, so fascinating when Randy or Clare opened it, was inaccessible to him. He understood how the door opened. He could put his paw on the magnetized strip – the indentation – between the body of the fridge and its door. What he could not do was open the door. He could not get a proper angle or produce the necessary torque when standing directly in front of the door. The kitchen cupboards were at first as inaccessible as the fridge, but Benjy hit on the idea of pushing a chair over to the counter. He jumped onto the chair, then onto the countertop. Standing up on the countertop, he was able to open the cupboard doors. Little good that did him, though. He could smell a number of things, but the bottom shelf of the cupboard was all he could reach. For all his trouble, the only things he managed to knock down were an opened bag of uncooked macaroni and a can of mushroom soup.

He ate the macaroni at once but the can of soup was no more than a toy to bat around.

The third and fourth days were dire. All speculation about dominance or dignity stopped. He understood at last that he had been abandoned – he *knew* it – and although the thought wounded him he put it aside. There was still water when he flushed the toilet. That was good. But he grew desperate for something solid. Remembering words that Majnoun had taught him, words that humans always responded to (said Majnoun), Benjy went to the front door and cried out.

– Help me! Help me!

For what seemed like days, he cried the words out. He spoke the words clearly and he was heard by a number of pedestrians. Unfortunately, circumstances conspired against the dog. To begin with, it was Halloween. Along Rhodes Avenue, a number of houses were done up in ghastly fashion. There were pumpkins on ledges, witches and zombies on lawns and porches. Some of the witches cackled as one approached them. Some of the zombies groaned loudly and moved their outstretched arms up and down. Given all that, Benjy's high-pitched calls for help were not alarming. Of those who heard his cries, a good number took his words for a witty reference to an old film in which a man is transformed into a fly.

It would have been better had Benjy simply barked. The sound of a dog in distress would not have amused anyone.

Other circumstances worked against him as well. Mr. Menzies, the landlord, had been called away to Glasgow, where his aging father had undergone heart surgery. The last thing on his mind was the property on Rhodes. It would be weeks before he so much as thought about it again. And finally: it being autumn, mice throughout the city were searching for winter homes. For every mouse that found a home, there were many more that found death in the sweet-tasting poisons left in corners or hidden in places a mouse might be forgiven for thinking safe. Before he had been called away and before Randy and Clare left without paying him back rent, Mr. Menzies had traps containing warfarin put down in mouse-tempting places throughout the house: behind appliances, in heating vents, in the cupboards beneath both the kitchen and the bathroom sinks. In principle, the traps were safe for domestic animals. Though the smell of the poison was alluring – like peanut butter, bacon and fried fish – there was no way for a cat or dog to open the black, plastic containers to get at the poisoned pellets. The traps should have been doubly safe, where Benjy was concerned, because something in their smell reminded him of a garden of death.

Desperately hungry at last, however, he opened the door to the cupboard beneath the kitchen sink. The cupboard smelled of chemicals and decay: soap, acids, rust, mould and grime. In amongst the chemical smells was a hint of peanut butter and fish skin. And it suddenly – or conveniently – occurred to Benjy that the smells of death came not from the plastic trap but from the tins, bottles and cans around it. If he could get the black container out, he would find the remains of a meal that had, by happy accident, been left under the sink.

As it happened, getting the trap from under the sink was not difficult. He burrowed amongst the bottles and cans, his sense of smell leading him to the black plastic container. What took time was deciding how best to open the thing. He could hear the 'food' rattling around inside. He could smell sustenance, but shaking the container did nothing. He was resourceful, however. After some thought, he dropped the trap from the kitchen counter, letting it fall to the floor. He did this only once. The box flew open and half a dozen pellets scattered like pink insects over the linoleum floor.

Benjy ate every one of the pellets. He waited, felt hungry still, then licked the floor where the pellets had touched. He was grateful that he had found food, strange-tasting food though it had been. He then repeated the process with the trap beneath the bathroom sink. After eating those, he drank water from the toilet and went to sleep on the bed.

True pain came late the following night. Benjy knew at once that he had made a mistake and that death was on him. His knowledge came from the strangeness of the agony: as if a fire were moving deliberately through the den of his body, searching for kindling. Also: his thirst was beyond appeal or satisfaction. His instinct was to stay still and hide from death. But he was driven to drink from the toilet, and this he did until he was too weak to stand up on his hind legs, too weak to drink.

The 'great cold' had come for Benjy. The death he experienced was as terrible as that suffered by Atticus, Rosie, Frick and Frack. And yet, in the midst of his terrible end, he experienced a stillness from which, in a manner of speaking, he could see beyond life and pain, beyond the world itself to a state that promised relief from suffering. As he died, bleeding from the nose, on the white tile floor of the bathroom, Benjy experienced a moment of hope that was not transcendent or mystical, but, rather, very much in keeping with his character. From the moment he was whelped, Benjy had been calculating, a schemer. But like all schemers he held within him the vision of a place or a state beyond schemes, where schemes were unnecessary because he was safe.

Benjy's greatest wish was for a place where the echelon was clear to all, where the powerful cared for the weak and the weak gave their respect without being coerced. He longed for balance, order, right and pleasure. It was this place that Benjy glimpsed as he died, and the glimpse brought him solace. Were it meaningful to speak of death as a state of being, one could say that Benjy died into hope itself.

In any case, he went to that place from which neither dogs nor men return.

Zeus had fulfilled Atticus's final wish. Benjy died a death as painful as Atticus's had been. Being the god of justice, however, Zeus had granted Benjy the same degree of hope that Atticus had had at *his* death.

All of this was no doubt interesting to some god somewhere, thought Hermes, but it was annoying. Had Benjy died happy or not? Thanks to their father's interference – and it was no use chiding him for it, either, there being no recourse from Zeus's will – the answer was not as clear as it might have been. Benjy's beatific vision of balance, order and right complicated matters. Apollo, of course, was certain that the dog had not died happy.

– Hope has nothing to do with happiness, Apollo had said
and there was no refuting that. Most of those who lived or died unhappily were as hope-filled as those whom the gods had favoured. Hope was a dimension of the mortal, nothing more. As he and Apollo discussed Benjy's death, however, it occurred to the god of thieves that he had not been clear-sighted when he'd dictated the terms of his and his brother's wager. The problem was death itself. No immortal could think of death without yearning for it. That yearning was, no doubt, what had led Hermes to imagine a happy death without being sufficiently clear as to the nature of the happiness.

– I think, he said to his brother, that we should broaden the definition of happiness. It would be generous of you to include hope or ...

Apollo cut him off.

– Are we suddenly human that we need to argue about words?
Hiding his thoughts, Hermes said

– No
but for the first time in all this business, he experienced something surprisingly like resentment.

4

MAJNOUN'S END

F ive years had passed, five years from the moment Hermes and
Apollo had entered the veterinary clinic and changed the dogs
they found there. Of the fifteen dogs, only two were left: Majnoun,
who was now eight, and Prince, who was seven.

Five years after Majnoun had come into her life, Nira thought
of him as her closest friend. Though they did not speak – or not
exactly – she felt that Majnoun understood her as well as her
husband did. Perhaps better. Over the years, there had been fewer
disagreements with Majnoun than with Miguel. But then, Miguel
was her mate. She hid nothing from him, nor he from her. Their
love was still strong, but it was mired in the day-to-day. With
Majnoun, Nira could be herself in a way that brought relief from
the company of her husband. It is a cruel irony, then, that a disagreement with Majnoun would prove disastrous for all three of them.

There had always been issues with Majnoun, of course. For
instance, Nira could not understand why he persisted in eating the
shit of other dogs. He knew that it upset her. On any number of
occasions she had begged him to control himself.

— It makes me ill to see you do it, she'd say.

Majnoun would nod and agree not to do it again, but, really, it was like asking a child not to eat any of the cakes left out at a patisserie. It was cruel to expect him to forbear, though out of consideration for her, Majnoun would forbear for months at a time until, inevitably, he'd forget her feelings and pounce on some fragrant deposit. So the whole cycle of revulsion (hers) and self-control (his) would begin again. This was a conflict that, Nira assumed, arose from Majnoun's nature. Majnoun was a dog, a sensitive and intelligent dog, but a dog just the same. For long stretches, she managed to convince herself he was other than what he was, then reminders of his nature would break the delusion.

There were other problems that, Nira assumed, had their origins in Majnoun's culture as opposed to his nature. For instance, she thought it distasteful for male dogs to mount females en masse, each waiting his turn. Majnoun did not even pretend to take her distaste seriously. A bitch in heat was a bitch in heat. There could be no argument about that and, as the bitches themselves wished it, he could not see why it shouldn't be done. She had to admit he had a point. She could imagine herself in heat, craving the friction of anonymous intercourse, but she was convinced that if she could influence Majnoun's attitude she might improve the life of female dogs by teaching Majnoun a respect he could pass on.

The line between natural (the things Majnoun couldn't help doing) and cultural (the things he could) was neither clear nor fixed. This was easy to forget in the heat of a dispute. It was just as easy to forget that Majnoun was not hers to improve. But, in any case, their fateful disagreement came over an idea that was impossible to put in one column (nature) or the other (culture), belonging as it did in both. More: it was an idea that mattered to Nira as much as it did to Majnoun: status.

As far as Majnoun was concerned, Miguel was the leader of their little pack. This thought annoyed Nira. She refused to allow that she was somehow subservient to her husband. There was no convincing Majnoun otherwise, however. He saw how she deferred to Miguel. He heard the echelon in their tones of voice (hers inevitably deferential), saw it in how they walked together or ate at the table. Their unequal status was so clear that it seemed to Majnoun as if Nira were trying to improve her station by feigning ignorance.

Majnoun's relationship to Miguel was nuanced, but not complex. He would have given his life for Nira, not Miguel. This was at least in part because Miguel was the head of their household and Majnoun looked to him for protection. Miguel, who did not believe Majnoun was gifted or unusual, would get down on the ground and play with Majnoun, pushing his head from side to side, chasing him, taking his chew toys away from him and throwing them about, roughly scratching Majnoun's belly and flanks. This was all, no doubt, undignified, but it was a pleasure to compete with Miguel for possession of a ball, to bark unselfconsciously when Miguel pushed him, to jump up on Miguel in a play at dominance. Nira tried to play with him, too, of course. She would throw the chewy, red ball around when they were outside, but you could tell her heart wasn't in it. She couldn't bring herself to say

– Go get it, boy! Go get it!

as if the ball were the most important thing on earth. For one thing, it seemed insulting to pretend that the ball mattered when she and Majnoun both knew it did not. In the end, Miguel was like a strong dog whom Majnoun both feared and admired, so he was offended when Nira questioned her husband's status.

Unfortunately, Nira would not leave the matter alone. One day, she asked whom he thought was next after Miguel, if Miguel was the, as she put it, 'grand high poobah.' This was, on the face of it, an offensive question, but her sneering tone was especially galling. As far as Majnoun was concerned, he and Nira were of equal status. Her question amounted to a denial of this. He let her know his feelings as forcefully as he could without attacking. He growled, his teeth bared, his tail lowered. It was a distressing moment for both of them, but Nira's question had been unspeakably rude. For days after their contretemps, Majnoun refused to acknowledge her presence, turning away from food she put down, leaving a room whenever she entered it. Nira realized that she had unwittingly gone too far, but he would not accept her apologies. For Majnoun, there seemed but two ways open to him: stay with someone who had challenged his status or leave for good. If he stayed, he would have to teach Nira to respect him. New to the ways of argument, he did not know how to do this without violence. But he would have died a thousand times rather than hurt Nira. And so, seeing no other way, Majnoun chose exile. He left the house without letting her know that he was gone for good.

This was the fateful moment, of course. A number of the gods having wagered on Majnoun's death, there was, on the part of those who wished him to die happy, interest in a reconciliation. Were it not for Zeus's edict, any number of them might have stepped in. As it was, none dared do anything openly. But Hermes, nursing his resentment, was upset by the impasse between Majnoun and Nira. He had intervened to save Prince, not Majnoun, but he was among those who believed Majnoun, at very least, *could* meet a good death.

– My poor, dear brother, said Apollo. There goes your last chance. The dog will be miserable without the woman, don't you agree?

– When it comes to mortals, answered Hermes, not even we know the future.

Apollo laughed.

– Spoken like a human, he said.

Though Hermes laughed, the insult stung. And so, despite his father's warning, the god of thieves and translators intervened in Majnoun's life. Dreams being his preferred medium, he appeared to Majnoun while the dog slept.

Majnoun had not gone far from home when he suddenly felt tired. He barely managed to find a safe place before he fell asleep. He began to dream at once.

He was in a meadow bounded on four sides by darkness. The meadow was covered in grass so green it looked painted. He himself was beneath a tree whose bole extended up as far as could be seen, disappearing into a single white cloud. The place was not frightening but it was somehow dangerous. Majnoun crouched down, ready to spring or to jump away from whatever came out of the darkness. What came was a poodle as black as he was but much more imposing.

– I haven't much time, said the dog.

It spoke no particular language. Its words were in Majnoun's mind, like a strange idea.

– You must not leave Nira. Your life is with her.

– I cannot go back, said Majnoun.

– I understand your predicament, but you have misinterpreted Nira's words. Humans do not think as you do.

– As *we* do, said Majnoun.

– As *you* do, said Hermes. I am one who wishes you well, but I am not a dog. Return to Nira. You will never misinterpret her words again, nor she yours.

– How can you know that? asked Majnoun.

– I have said it and so it will be, answered Hermes.

With that, the dream ended and Majnoun woke. He was on a lawn near High Park, not far from the arched entrance on Parkside, not far from where the streetcars turn around. Majnoun had had dreams before, of course, but none had ever been as vivid. He could recall its every detail and, despite himself, he wondered if he'd been dreaming at all.

The answer came soon enough. Walking along Parkside, Majnoun was assaulted by music coming from a car radio that was turned up loud. Majnoun heard the words

> In the golden tent of early morning
> when the sky has turned its back
> when the sky has turned its back and isn't listening
> when the scallops stand upright on their hinges . . .

Then the car took off and he could no longer make the lyrics out.

There was nothing unusual about the loud music. Men in automobiles often tried to hurt one with noise. But Majnoun suddenly *understood* the lyrics, mysterious though they were. He understood that lyrics were not meaningful the way human words usually are, that lyrics were a ground where sense, rhythm and melody engaged. At times, sense won out; at times, rhythm; at times, melody. At times, the three things were at war, the way emotion, instinct and intelligence were at war within him. At times, the three were in harmony. The lyrics he'd heard suddenly struck him as a brilliant skirmish and, like someone who finally gets a joke, Majnoun sat and laughed, laughing as Benjy once had: gasping for breath while a feeling of pleasure escaped from him.

Nor did his newly acquired understanding stop there. Majnoun found, as he walked in High Park, that he could easily recognize the intent behind words he overheard. He was amazed, for instance, to hear a woman say to the man beside her

— I'm sorry, Frank. I just can't go on anymore …

her words an attempt to comfort and wound at the same time. How complex and vicious humans were! And how strange to suddenly appreciate the depths of their feelings. Whereas previously, he had thought them stunted, clumsy and unwilling to grasp the obvious, Majnoun now realized humans were almost as deep as dogs, though in their own particular way.

Wishing to see if he would understand Nira in this way, he returned home.

He had not been gone long, two hours at most. The back door was still unlocked. He stood on his hind legs, pushed down on the handle's metal thumb-piece. The door opened and he went in. There, as if waiting for him, was Nira.

— Jim, she said. I thought you'd left us.

Majnoun caught every nuance. He caught her contrition, her worry, her affection for him, her sadness, her relief that he had returned, her confusion at speaking this way to a dog. It was, of course, impossible for him to respond to so many nuances at once.

— I have been called Majnoun for much of my life, he said. It is the name my first master gave me and it is the one I prefer.

He spoke clearly and Nira understood. She was so used to understanding him without words, however, that she did not at first realize he'd spoken. She had the odd but fleeting sensation that Majnoun had entered her consciousness in some new way.

— I'm sorry, Majnoun, she said at last. I didn't know.

Hermes's gift to Majnoun was precious and unprecedented, but it was also something of a burden. From being a dog who knew English fairly well, Majnoun became one who understood all human languages. Walking in Roncesvalles, he sometimes had to stop himself from listening to conversation in Polish, say

— *Te pomidory są zgniłe!*

or Hungarian

— *Megőrültél?*

Hearing other languages was like hearing new rhythms, melodies and reasons. At times, he found himself so transfixed that Nira had to call him from his reveries.

— Maj, come on. We've got things to do.

(Majnoun's favourite human language was English. There was no doubt about that. This had little to do with the fact he'd learned English first. It was that English, of all the languages he experienced, was the one best suited to dogs. A dog had to think differently in English, yes, but the sounds and rhythms of English were those that best mimicked the rhythms and tonal range of a dog's natural tongue. One pleasant consequence of Majnoun's love for English – pleasant for him and for Nira – was his taking up of poetry. With Prince's poems as his model, Majnoun 'wrote' the same way Prince had, memorizing his poems. Then he'd recite them to Nira.

> In China, where wild dogs are eaten,
> I am dismayed to be in season.
> I curse men who think of me as food
> and dream of rickshaws, and lacquered wood.

Or again:

> If rackabones eat up the sky,
> if words spring out of rock,
> my soul will wind down
> and life run out the clock.

On the other hand, when Nira asked him which language he liked best, Majnoun did not say English. He could not. As far as Majnoun was concerned, the language of dogs was more expressive, more vivid, easier to understand and more beautiful than any human speech. He tried to teach her Dog, but, to his surprise, their efforts foundered on Nira's inability to tell the difference between a bark of pleasure and a call for attention, a crucial distinction in canine speech. Nira was disappointed. The only phrase she learned passably well was 'I will bite you,' not something you could say to just any dog. She would have liked to speak to him in his own tongue, but the truth was: Majnoun could not abide her accent and was not unhappy when she stopped trying.)

Majnoun's decision to speak was not, at first, welcomed by Nira. True, their friendship was restored when Majnoun returned home and spoke. But it was unsettling to speak English with him. The two of them had evolved a lovely, wordless communication in which silence, the turn of a head or a hesitant nod were all meaningful. Now she had to deal with those things as well as words and, in the beginning, she found Majnoun more arduous to comprehend, though her understanding was deeper. More than that: Majnoun's speaking brought what Nira thought of as 'procedural problems.' They both agreed it was best if Nira alone knew of his ability to speak. But as they grew more comfortable with each other, one or the other would, in public, forget their compact and ask a question or comment on something. When it was Nira who spoke to Majnoun, there was naturally less confusion than when Majnoun spoke to her. Majnoun's voice was lower than Nira's, so bystanders who heard his voice had trouble deciding whence exactly the words had come. This confusion brought unwanted attention.

Then there was Miguel. Miguel did not particularly like Majnoun. He'd preferred Benjy and he resented the closeness Nira and Majnoun shared. Majnoun understood all of this and forgave Miguel because Miguel's feelings were, as far as Majnoun was concerned, honourable. Still, it was clear that Miguel might not have Majnoun's best interests in mind, that he might not protect Majnoun the way Nira would. So Nira and Majnoun agreed that it would be best if they did not speak in front of Miguel. This meant that, at times, Miguel's presence made the two feel awkward. It made Nira feel as if she were betraying her husband's trust, while Majnoun felt he was betraying the pack leader.

In the end, it took Nira some time to feel at ease with Majnoun's English. Once she was accustomed to it, however, his presence became so precious to her that the fact Majnoun was a dog ceased to signify. It stopped occurring to her that he was not as she was. Really, what did it matter that Majnoun was a dog while, for instance, they sat together by the Boulevard Club watching the willows move?

(Willows were for both of them a source of fascination. Though he knew better, Majnoun had always thought the trees were a subtle kind of animal, deceptive and imperious. To the very end, part of him still believed it. He could not contemplate the swaying branches without wishing to bite them. Minus the desire to bite, Nira felt something similar. For her the trees were like mammoths in leaf: ancient, slow, the last of something imperial, though of course they were not. They were only trees.)

Perfect understanding between beings is no guarantor of happiness. To perfectly understand another's madness, for instance, is to be mad oneself. The veil that separates earthly beings is, at times, a tragic barrier, but it is also, at times, a great kindness. In fact, the only beings to achieve 'perfect mutual understanding' are the gods. For the gods, *any* emotion or state of mind – madness, anger, bitterness, etc. – is pleasurable, so understanding is neither here nor there.

Hermes knew all this. As the god of translators, he was also the god of *mis*translation and *mis*understanding. It was he who, in a manner of speaking, muddied waters that became too clear or clarified those that had grown murky. But if there was ever a being who could be made happy by the gift of understanding, it was Majnoun. The more Majnoun understood of Nira, the more grateful he was that he had returned to what was now, undoubtedly, his home.

Two years passed.

As he grew older and more statesmanlike, Majnoun came to appreciate Nira in the best way possible: through the things that she loved. Her films, for instance. How deeply she admired *Cléo from 5 to 7*, *Days of Heaven* and *Tokyo Story*! *Tokyo Story* above all. One afternoon, Nira sat with him and they watched the movie together. It was the first time Majnoun had watched any film all the way through. It wasn't that he was not interested in films. It was that he could not stand to see so many distant worlds without being able to smell them. Worlds were not real without their odours, so movies and paintings were inevitably a disappointment. But Nira so loved *Tokyo Story* that he sat still for the two hours it took to watch it.

When the movie was over, it took a moment for Nira to regain her composure. As always, she was moved to tears when Setsuko Hara cries.

— Did you like it? she asked at last.

— Yes, said Majnoun.

— You didn't think it was too long? Some people find it boring.

— It was not boring, said Majnoun, but it was strange. The people were always looking away to where you couldn't see. The whole time, I thought there was something coming. Then at the end, it was death that came.

It touched Nira that Majnoun could appreciate something she cherished. But there were aspects of the film that Majnoun found difficult to interpret, despite Hermes's gift. To begin with, there was the general absence of dogs. When, somewhere toward the middle of the film, four dogs ran across the screen, responding to the whistled call of their master, Majnoun was immediately alert. So, it was something of a disappointment that the dogs were never seen again. But then, somewhere toward the end of the film, a man whistles for dogs who are not shown. First, the one who whistles is invisible. Then, it's the ones who are called. These two moments, unexplained, seemed to Majnoun like a metaphysical puzzle at the heart of the film.

Also intriguing was all the bowing. The association of height and status did not, of course, faze him. If anything, it made the Japanese seem noble. But where were the ones who made themselves big? That was the question. With so many people bowing down, it seemed to Majnoun like a competition amongst the low to see who could be lowest. In which case, discretion was strength, a paradox that Majnoun found almost as compelling as the film's relative absence of dogs.

In the end, it occurred to Majnoun that the two mysteries might be related. Dogs being capable of bowing much lower than humans, it perhaps followed that, in *Tokyo Story*, the dogs were a mysterious power it was forbidden to show too often, that a glimpse of them was all the discreet filmmakers had allowed themselves. Understandably, this idea contributed to Majnoun's affection for the film.

It was even more interesting to read Nira's favourite books. There was more time to think about things. Nira read *Pride and Prejudice* and *Mansfield Park* to him over the space of a month, aloud in the late afternoons before Miguel came home from work. Of these two, *Mansfield Park* was the one that troubled Majnoun most. It seemed to him almost frightening in its rage for order, like a manual for masters.

When they'd finished reading it, Majnoun said
– Nira, do you like fucking?
(*Fucking* was one of Miguel's words. Nira had never spoken it.)
When she'd recovered from her surprise at the question, Nira said
– Where did *that* come from, Maj?
– I was thinking about Fanny Price, said Majnoun. She loves Edmund but she disapproves of fucking, doesn't she?

– It's impossible to say. As I see it, Fanny thinks there's a right time and place for everything. But, to answer your question, I prefer making love. Look … this is a very personal matter, Maj, but there are times when I miss Miguel and I like being with him and I like when being with him turns into something more. It's slow and it takes time. If you only saw the last part, you might think there's no difference between making love and fucking, but there is for me. But then there are other times when I really just want him inside me and it's almost as if it doesn't matter that it's Miguel, but it *does* matter.

– I see, said Majnoun

but here, too, his understanding of the human situation – as opposed to his understanding of Nira – was coloured by his lack of familiarity with certain rituals. He himself had never 'made love,' nor could he imagine wishing to.

What was interesting to him was how much humans relied on their imaginations. Not just for amusement but for fundamental things as well. He preferred to allow his body to think for him. Or he had in the old days before he'd changed. Now that he was somewhere between dog and human, he was curious about the imagination. Had he not been (as Nira called it) 'neutered,' he thought he might at least have tried to 'make love' to another dog. But then again, it would have been difficult to know where to start. Bitches in heat – the very smell of them an indescribably pleasing derangement – wanted fucking. There was no place for what Nira called 'seduction.' He briefly considered if bringing food to a bitch *out* of heat might put her *in* heat, but why would he bother? He was certainly not what Nira called 'heterosexual,' but neither was he homosexual or even bisexual. There were times when he was aroused in the presence of other dogs or humans or plush toys, for that matter, and he would mount them or rub against them if he could. On that score, he certainly made no distinction between bitches and non-bitches. As had happened after they'd watched *Tokyo Story*, Majnoun was left with a kind of pleasing puzzlement when they'd finished reading *Mansfield Park*.

In the end, it surprised Majnoun to discover that works of art –
Tokyo Story, *Mansfield Park*, Mahler's Fourth Symphony, and so on –
were not understandable in the way people were. These works were, it
seemed, created to evade understanding while inviting it. He came to
love this aspect of the human, which was, of course, an aspect of Nira.

Nira's and Majnoun's path to understanding was mutually taken.
Nira learned what was important to Majnoun as he learned what
was important to her. Their journeys were quite different, however.
To begin with, there were no artefacts for her to consider. No films
or books that Majnoun loved. No music. Moreover, there was an
asymmetry in their sensory capacities. Majnoun's vision was not as
keen as hers, but he noticed things she did not: squirrels, for instance.
Majnoun could detect their slightest movement, were the creatures
up in the trees or somewhere in the distance. His sense of smell was
astounding. He could tell whether or not she had put shadow benny
in her stewed chicken. And his sense of taste was just as impressive.
Finally, his hearing was more acute than hers. He could hear higher
pitches than she could, naturally. But he interpreted sounds differently as well. Nira had always heard that Bach's music (among her
favourites) was loved by all animals. Not by Majnoun it wasn't. Not
at all. For Majnoun, Bach's music was like having needles prick you
from the inside. He preferred Wagner – whose music Nira disliked–
and he loved Anton Bruckner.

– Do dogs have stories? Nira asked him one day.

– Of course, said Majnoun.

– Oh, Maj! said Nira. Please tell me one.

Majnoun agreed and began:

– There is the smell of bitch, but I am before a wall. The smell is
strong and I am going mad. I can't eat. I can't drink. The wall is too
thick to knock down and it goes for miles in this direction and for
miles in that direction. I dig under and I dig and I dig. The master
cannot see my digging so I dig until there is air beneath the wall and
the smell of bitch is stronger than it was before. I call to the bitch
but there is no answer. But there is air beneath the wall. Should I go

on digging? I don't know, but I dig even though I can smell the master's food from his house. The smell of bitch is stronger and stronger. I call out, but now I am hungry.

Here Majnoun stopped.

– Is that it? asked Nira.

– Yes, said Majnoun. Do you not like it?

– Well, it's ... different, said Nira. But it doesn't really have an ending.

– It has a very moving ending, said Majnoun. Is it not sad to be caught between desires?

By degrees, the distance between Nira and Majnoun narrowed until each could anticipate what the other wanted. Nira could tell when exactly Majnoun wished to eat or go for a walk. Majnoun knew when it was time to leave Nira alone, when it was time to comfort her, when it was time to sit quietly by her side. By degrees, they had less use for words or English.

One morning, they discovered that they'd dreamed of the same field, the same clouds, the same house in the distance – wooden with a red-brick chimney. They had dreamed of the same squirrels and rabbits. They had drunk from the same clear stream. There was only one difference: when Nira, in her dream, looked into the water, she saw Majnoun's face reflected back at her, while Majnoun, in his, saw Nira's face where his should have been. The fact of this shared dream was so moving to Nira that, ever after, she refused to allow anyone – even Miguel – to refer to Majnoun as 'her' dog.

– I'm as much his as he's mine, she'd insist.

Her friends – and her husband – thought this an annoying eccentricity. Majnoun knew what she meant – that she was not his master – and he was grateful. But in his heart he felt as if he *did* belong to her, in the sense that he was a part of Nira and she a part of him.

What neither could have known was that their shared and simple dream was a harbinger of disaster. They had now grown so close that Atropos, the Fate who cuts the thread of a mortal's life, could not tell their threads apart. Majnoun's time to die had come — he was fairly old, for a dog — but she could not cut his thread without the risk of cutting Nira's.

The work of the three sisters — Clotho, Lachesis and Atropos — is generally straightforward. The first spins the thread of a life. The second draws out the length of thread each being will have. The third cuts the thread and ends that being's time on earth. It often happens that life threads are intertwined — most commonly, the lives of husbands and wives, which is why they often die together or close together in time. And, in fact, Nira's and Miguel's threads were almost as closely intertwined as Nira's and Majnoun's. Though Nira and Miguel were meant to live longer than Majnoun, the threads of all three lives were so wound up, so similar in hew and thickness, that Atropos was not certain whose life would end if she used her scissors.

She complained bitterly to Zeus that one or more of the gods must have interfered with the mortals because it was unnatural that she could not properly end a life she was meant to end. Zeus, who disliked the Fates and avoided speaking with them, was unmoved.

– A life must end, he said. It is your duty to cut the thread. Do your duty.

Spitefully, Atropos cut two of the three lives that were wound together, then added years to the one that was left by way of balance. Clotho and Lachesis giggled at her daring, but Atropos was too contemptuous to share in their laughter.

– King of the gods! she said to Lachesis. 'Loud-mouthed fornicator' is more like it. Let him just try to get back at me for this!

For a week, Nira and Miguel had been arguing about the dishes. Miguel always did them, but he did not, he felt, receive the credit he deserved.

To Majnoun, it was a strange argument. To begin with, Miguel never allowed Nira to do the dishes. He would insist that he was not some 'male chauvinist' who didn't do housework, though in fact the dishes was all he did, where housework was concerned. Nira's point was that she never got credit for doing the cleaning, the tidying and the cooking, but she never complained about that. As occasionally happened, Miguel alluded to her work – copy editing – with a certain contempt, as if it weren't quite 'work.' Copy editing allowed her to stay at home, and some part of him resented this, given that he, a script editor for various programs at TV Ontario, had to leave every morning. They argued about dishes, then housework, then work, then housework, then dishes, then housework, then work and so on. It was astounding, to Majnoun, that a runaround like that could go on for so long. More: although housework was the basis of an argument that flared up every six months or so, both were always as upset by the subject as if it were something new.

'Housework' was a strange concept in any case. As long as one didn't shit in inconvenient places, where was the problem? As far as Majnoun was concerned, the real trouble was with the size of human dens and with the fastidiousness of primates. You would think, having as much space as they did, that they would simply move from one room to another when they wished, but their need for chemical smells and clean surfaces betrayed them. As for the dishes: what was the point of cleaning off the smells and tastes that clung to bowls, pots and plates? That was like scrubbing the best part away, then congratulating yourself for it. To think that poor Nira got so worked up about these things!

Though he did not like to intrude on what was, clearly, an episode in the struggle for dominance, it occurred to Majnoun that what Miguel and Nira needed was to spend time together, without him around, that a change of routine would do them good. Nira was sceptical. She and Miguel had never been ones for travel. They preferred things nearby: plays, movies or restaurants. Besides which, their happiest times had come when they were home. Nira had had enough of arguing with Miguel, however, and Miguel, not coincidentally, had had enough of arguing with her. So, when Nira suggested that they visit a few wineries together and spend two nights (Friday and Saturday) near Thirty Bench, Miguel agreed at once. Anything to end the bickering.

But who would take care of Majnoun?

Majnoun, who could open the fridge if he needed something, who did not mind if she put out a bag of dry 'dog food,' who shat in the toilet as humans did, who could get out of the house if there was fire or smoke, who could turn the backyard tap on and off if he needed water, shook his head. He wanted no strange company. Nira wasn't comfortable with the idea of leaving him on his own. But Miguel – who assumed the dog would be locked safely inside – said

– Majnoun will be fine.

Behind him, Majnoun nodded in agreement, so that, despite her misgivings, Nira relented. Then, Friday came.

That morning, Nira and Majnoun went for a walk together. It had been some time since they'd been to High Park, because Majnoun – now ten – could not stand the proximity of other dogs and could not defend himself as well as he once could. They decided to walk in the park but away from the off-leash areas, going in through the iron-and-stone gate at High Park and Parkside. They were more or less alone, there being few people or dogs about. When they came to Centre Road, they followed it around the curve and up the hill, talking – for no particular reason – about the seasons. Nira mentioned that her favourite season was autumn. She loved the way the trees changed colour, the cool weather, the coming of winter. Majnoun did not know that one could have a favourite season.

– You must like one more than the others, said Nira.

– I cannot think why, said Majnoun. I am never sure when the seasons begin and I like in between the seasons, too, and in between in between and in between in between in between.

Here, they both laughed. Not, as was sometimes the case, because Majnoun had been inadvertently amusing, but because he was teasing her.

– There should be a hundred seasons, said Majnoun.

— You're right, said Nira

and she scratched the place behind his ear, which was a feeling that Majnoun loved.

They had walked for longer than usual, for an hour or more. They had left the park and strolled along Sorauren all the way to Pearson, where, though she didn't like to indulge her cravings, Nira bought a carrot muffin at Mitzi's and, as if to make Majnoun her accomplice, gave him some.

— It's too sweet, said Majnoun.

— Yes, but it's got carrots and, besides, we don't eat them every day.

Once home, Nira had packed the little she needed: toiletries, makeup, a black dress, a change of underwear. Together, they had listened to part of *La Clemenza di Tito*. Time passed and Miguel returned home from work. Not half an hour later, Miguel and Nira were leaving. As Miguel took their suitcases to the car, Nira crouched to look Majnoun in the eyes, a thing that always made him uncomfortable.

— You're sure you'll be okay? she asked. I left the bag of dry food out, in case you get hungry. There's more in the pantry. There's steak in the fridge on the bottom shelf. I made sure the tap outside was oiled. You shouldn't have any trouble if you get thirsty. Are you sure you'll be okay?

— Yes, he said.

At times like this, he preferred Miguel's attitude. Miguel was not as caring as Nira, but neither did he make Majnoun nervous.

Nira ran her fingers through the hair on Majnoun's flank.

— We'll be back Sunday afternoon, she said.

Then she was gone, the last sounds he heard being her key in the front door and her fading footsteps as she walked off the porch.

A day passed. And then another.

As previously noted, one of the worst aspects of the dogs' change in intelligence was their new consciousness of time. The state of bliss in which one moment is a thousand and a thousand moments one was something all the dogs had taken for granted. After the change, each of the fifteen had had to fend for themselves against a new Time, a Time that knew how to make its passage felt. Majnoun had done better than most, because he'd had Nira to help him lose track of moments that passed. Walking with Nira along Roncesvalles or by the lakeshore was time that he would happily have prolonged. If anything, their hours together passed too quickly. With Nira gone, however, there was little to protect him from the excruciation that duration can be. To keep himself occupied in the first twenty-four hours, he had written a poem for Nira, something to surprise her with on her return.

> Summer is full of smoke,
> and endless lawns. Quietly,
> whether across moss or on algae,
> knee over the railing of the little porch,
> fate comes.

Then, as Nira had left *Tannhäuser* in the CD player for him, he'd listened to the opera, slept, listened to it again, gone outside and wandered around the edges of High Park away from people and dogs, slept, listened to *Tannhäuser* again, slept again. On Monday morning, he woke and was confused to find himself alone. The kitchen clock seemed to be working – the second hand jumped as it always did – but Nira had not returned. This was as strange as if the sun had risen in the west. He ate little that day. And though he knew Miguel and Nira did not like it, he lay down in their bed, the place in the house where the smell of them was strongest.

If Monday was bewildering, Tuesday was strange beyond language. Some time in the afternoon, he heard a key turn in the front door. The sound made him immediately alert. Someone was trying to invade their home. He knew the rhythms, the voices, the very weight of both Nira and Miguel. Neither of them was at the door. He ran to the front hall growling, ready to attack whoever entered. But he did not attack. *Could* not. The intruder was someone familiar but 'wrong,' and Majnoun could not help himself.

– Who are you? he asked.

The man – Miguel's brother – stood a moment staring at Majnoun before pushing the door wide open. To the people behind him, he said

– Christ! That was weird. I could have sworn the dog spoke.

Behind him, someone said

– Nothing's right without Miguel here.

Majnoun could barely keep himself from attacking the man who'd spoken Miguel's name. It seemed to him that no one else had the right to make such an important sound. He retreated into the house, however, moving backwards, tail down, to let Miguel's family in.

No sooner did she enter the house than Miguel's mother began to weep.

– Oh lors! she cried.

Her sons held her up and the four of them remained in the front hall, huddled together. Their emotion – which Majnoun experienced as if it were his own – provoked the most conflicting feelings: pity, dislike and resentment. Why should these people be here instead of Nira? Nor did they look like leaving any time soon. They took their time in the front hall, the men finally helping the old woman into the living room, where she collapsed on the sofa, still overcome by emotion.

What a strange invasion it was. No one paid the least attention to him. No one spoke. They went through the house at a funereal pace, looking for whatever: clothes, letters, boxes. Miguel's brothers did most of the searching, until their mother found the strength to rise from the sofa and help them look. Majnoun remained in the living room, sitting quietly, unmoving. It was a kind of torture not to speak, not to ask when Nira was coming home.

– What about the dog? said one of the brothers.

– Maybe Sarah will take it, said another.

– It was Nira's dog, said Miguel's mother. One of her friends should have it.

Those were all the words Majnoun needed to hear. He understood at once that Miguel's family were nothing to do with him, that they were unfaithful to Nira, and that they meant him no good. With a minimum of fuss or urgency, he rose from where he was sitting and walked away from them. Once in the kitchen, he opened the back door, crossed the yard, opened the back fence and, before anyone so much as thought to stop him, he was halfway along Geoffrey, heading toward Roncesvalles. From there he went into High Park, returning to what had once been his pack's den, the only place left to him, though it was haunted by the spirits of dogs who were gone.

Early the next morning, Majnoun's vigil began a new phase. He returned to the house and warily waited for Nira, choosing a vantage across the street, far enough away that he could run, if he had to, but near enough to see all the comings and goings.

Over the years that followed, Majnoun had much time to wonder if he'd been hasty running out when he had. Perhaps, if he'd stayed, he might have overheard something about Nira, about her where-abouts. Not that hearsay would have changed the course of his life. Whatever Miguel's family might have said, Majnoun would likely have done what he did in any case. That is, wait for Nira.

The beginning of waiting was, in its way, complicated. Not the decision to wait. No real decision was necessary. He knew he would wait for Nira because Nira would return. It would have been unthink-ably cruel to force Nira to search for him. But waiting itself required that he make a number of choices. He had to eat, for instance. Belonging to Nira in the way he did, he could not allow himself to die, though he resented the time needed to keep himself fed because it was time spent away from the place Nira would expect him to be. Most mornings, he scrounged in High Park, eating whatever he happened upon. If he was still hungry, he waited until the place that sold squeeze toys and dog food opened: the Kennel Café. There, they inevitably put out biscuits and a bowl of water. More than enough to keep him going for a day.

Then there was the strategy of waiting.

In the beginning, the place was overrun by Miguel's family. Whenever one of them saw Majnoun, they'd run after him. Why they wanted him at all was unclear. They seemed to think he was theirs. But he'd be off before they finished plotting their course. He'd run half a block, wait to see if they'd followed, run off half a block more, and so on until they gave up. It hurt his old bones to run, but he would not be caught.

Also in the beginning, he could not a find a place that hid him while allowing him to look out for Nira. Whenever he stayed in any one place for too long, there was inevitably a human there to disturb him. The closest he came to capture was when someone called the Toronto Animal Services to come and get him. Animal Services, he knew, were serious business. Nira had warned him about them. They killed inconvenient dogs. So, no sooner did he see the Animal Services van than he was off, darting behind houses, hiding, slinking, hiding until he made High Park, where he hid in the coppice for two whole days, two whole days away from home, worried that Nira would come or that she had already come and was upset that he was not there.

His life changed. The waiting changed.

Interest in Majnoun died down with the 'For Sale' sign that appeared on the lawn of he, Miguel and Nira's home. Evidently, Miguel's family were selling what did not belong to them. In a matter of weeks, the sign came down and strangers began to enter and leave his home: a woman, a man, two small children with blond hair.

Rather than staying on any one lawn or waiting in any one place, Majnoun varied his vantage points: across the street, two houses down, one house down, and even – once he was certain the woman and her children were not violent – in the backyard that had been his. As the years passed and he grew older and thinner, Majnoun learned to worry a little less that he might miss Nira's return. He grew more confident that Nira would look for him when she came home and, what's more, that he would know she was looking. When she came back, he would know it.

As his life settled into a routine, the world slowly changed around him. Two years after Nira had gone, the people on Geoffrey began to leave food out for him: a piece of meat or chicken, bread, carrots, whatever was leftover from their own meals. They kept their distance, because Majnoun was still a little intimidating (black with some grey, inscrutable, alert), but no one ever called the Toronto Animal Services again. The dogs in the area left him alone as well. Not out of fear, not because he was unnatural, but because the purity of his attention commanded respect. No dog could have doubted or misunderstood Majnoun's resolve or the depths of his longing. They all knew what it was like to wait and, every once in a while, one would join Majnoun, silently sitting at a slight remove, sharing his task as a mark of respect.

To keep himself alert as he waited, Majnoun thought about things. Over the years, he thought about a thousand things, but two questions occupied most of his time. The first was about humanity. What, he wondered, did it mean to be human? The question was, ultimately, impossible for him to answer. He had been born outside of the human and, so, was ignorant of the implications of a world created by their limitations. What would it be like, for instance, to be unable to distinguish the smell of snow in winter from the smell of snow in early spring? What kind of world was it in which one could not, blindfolded, distinguish the great range in the taste of water or smell when a female was in heat? To be so limited? Inconceivable. And, of course, it was impossible to know a state (to know the human) by subtracting things in oneself, as if 'human' were what is left once the best of dog has been taken away.

This question was a way to think about what made Nira Nira, to try to imagine the world as she saw it, to feel it as she felt it, to think about it as she might.

The second question was about himself and what it meant – if it meant anything at all – to be a dog. What was he, really? Where did he fit in the world? Was he waiting for Nira because it was in his nature to wait, or was his dedication unique and noble? Most days, he felt only that waiting was right. Every once in a while, however, he imagined waiting was only the expression of an instinct, something he had to do. This thought, whenever it occurred, saddened him, mere instinct being unworthy of Nira, who was not his master but, rather, a being who completed him, made him more than he would otherwise have been.

And so, speculating about the canine brought him closer to Nira as well.

Though it is far from obvious, the gods are not inevitably indifferent to the suffering of mortals. At times, mortal suffering is amusing to them, at times diverting; at times, though rarely, it is touching.

When Majnoun's vigil had lasted five years, Zeus allowed himself to notice that the dog had lived well beyond its span, that its suffering was unnecessarily prolonged. Moved by the dog's nobility of spirit, he visited the hall of the Fates.

No one enjoys visiting the Fates. They are haughty and beyond petition. They are eccentric in their views, and the hall where mortal lives are spun is itself unpleasant: white, exactly one millimetre less than infinite in length, ten metres tall and ten metres wide. Eleven white urns – each filled with the essence of a particular emotion – sit in a row near Clotho's spinning wheel. As a life is spun, it is dipped in each of the urns by Lachesis before being cut by Atropos. (In principle, Lachesis dips each and every thread in each of the jars, assuring that every life has the same generous emotional range. Lachesis is unpredictable, however, dipping some threads in one or two emotions alone, rendering a life monotonous or unbearable. It is through Lachesis that suicides are born.)

Given their mansion and their personalities, it is not surprising that most of the gods avoided them entirely, that the sisters had only each other for company. So, it was with a mixture of secret pleasure and open defiance that Clotho, Lachesis and Atropos received Zeus into their hall.

– I hope you haven't come to blame us for anything, said Atropos.

– I have known you since the beginning of time, said Zeus. You've never been anything but blameless.

– He's right, said Clotho. We do what no other immortals can do. We *must* be blameless.

The sisters laughed.

– And yet, said Zeus, your tasks are not always rightly done. It seems some mortals have had their lifespans shortened while others have had them prolonged.

– The king of the gods must be at fault, said Atropos, if an injustice has been committed.

– It isn't I who decided to extend Majnoun's life, said Zeus. You three have drawn out the suffering of an innocent being. You have interfered where I expressly forbade it. But I'm sure you have your reasons and I'd be honoured if you shared them with me.

– Fuck you, said Atropos.

– If the being you refer to is suffering, said Clotho, talk to your sons about it. They've always been meddlers. I'm sure you'll find they're to blame, though some might blame you since you're unable to control your children, O great and powerful Zeus.

Zeus bowed his head.

– The least you could do, he said, is end Majnoun's suffering.

– That we will not do, said Atropos. It is out of our hands and yours.

– Would you have him wait forever?

– It won't be forever, said Lachesis. The dog is not immortal.

– Fifty years at most, said Clotho.

– That is a long time for a dog, said Zeus.

Atropos, who had, despite herself, been moved by Majnoun's fidelity to Nira, relented.

– If you can convince the creature to give up his wait, we will allow his life to end. Perhaps next time we come to you for advice, you will listen.

Having got all he could from the Fates, Zeus summoned Hermes and Apollo.

— This game of yours has cost me more than it has cost you two, he said. One of you will convince Majnoun to give up his vigil. If you fail, both of you will suffer until his suffering ends.

— There's no need to threaten us, Father, said Apollo. Haven't we always been good sons? We'll do whatever you ask.

Which is how, after Zeus's sons had fought about it and Apollo had alluded to Hermes's well-known tendency to meddle in mortal lives through dreams, Hermes was tasked with setting Majnoun free. As to their wager, both gods agreed that Majnoun could not, without Nira, die happy. Prince – himself on the verge of death – was Hermes's last remaining hope.

— You know, I'm looking forward to the years of servitude you'll owe me, said Apollo. We'll see how you like being chauffeur to a ball of fire.

By allowing Nira and Majnoun a divine intimacy, Hermes had made his task more difficult than it might have been. It was no use simply asking Majnoun to abandon his vigil. He did not have the rhetorical skill needed to convince the dog that Nira would not return. The god of thieves was further hampered by his admiration for Majnoun. He would not consider obvious trickery. He would not disguise himself as Nira, for instance. And yet, knowing that Majnoun could not be happy without Nira, knowing that Majnoun's vigil was futile, Hermes had incentive to accomplish this small mercy: to allow Majnoun to accept his own death.

One day, as Majnoun sat in the yard opposite the house that had been his home, a black poodle – almost Majnoun's double, save that this one had bright blue eyes – greeted him in the language of his pack.

— Do you mind if I sit with you? Hermes asked.

Pleased to hear the language of his pack, Majnoun said

— I do not mind, but how do you know our language?

— I am well-travelled, said Hermes, I know many languages.

— Even the human ones?

– Yes, said Hermes, I have lived many places.

In English, Majnoun said

– You must be very intelligent.

In English, Hermes answered

– I am, but I don't like to talk about my virtues.

Majnoun knew then that this was the being he had seen in dreams.

– You are not a dog, he said. I know you. What do you want with me?

– I am here to help.

– Tell me where Nira is, said Majnoun.

– I can take you to her, said Hermes, but you will have to leave this place.

Majnoun looked over at the house he had been contemplating for five years: red brick, tall chimney, pyramid roof, a window with shutters on the third floor, a bay window on the second floor, front porch with its own roof, blue spruce in the front yard, different kinds of bushes that served as a hedge. You might almost have said that he loved its bricks, aluminium and wood, but, of course, they were precious only because Nira had lived within.

– I cannot leave, said Majnoun.

Hermes said

– Then I will keep you company, if you'll allow it. Is there anything I can do for you?

Majnoun considered the question. There was nothing he wanted, but he was curious about the visitor's influence.

– Make time stop, he said.

– It is very unpleasant, said Hermes, but as you wish.

And time stood still. A bird that had alighted on the branch of a tree two doors down stopped singing but went on producing the same note it had produced at the moment time stopped. No sound having had time to decay, the noise around them was unbearable, the earth a deafening alarm. A butterfly hovering above the leaves of a flowering shrub seemed stuck in a jelly of air, the light-blue dots on its wings clearly visible above a yellow fringe. Even the smells stood still, so that when Majnoun moved his head ever so slightly, he could smell a vein of scent and then another and another, each scent like a layer in mica.

— That's enough, said Majnoun
only moments after time had stopped.

— I used to amuse myself doing that, said Hermes. It was a test to see how long I could last. I am like you, Majnoun. I never lasted long. My brother Ares could take it for days, though.

— Your brother must be strong, said Majnoun.

— No, said Hermes. The noise reminds him of war, and he likes it.
At that, Majnoun understood how completely his companion transcended the world. Though he was intimidated, he asked

— What is it like to be a god?

— I am very sorry, said Hermes, but the only language in which I can truly express this is one that mortals cannot learn.

— Do you feel as we do? asked Majnoun.

— No, said Hermes. For me, what you call feeling is of a different order and nature. It is palpable, like steam or smoke.

— How strange, said Majnoun.

For a time, the two sat quietly together, contemplating the houses, the sky, and the world. The people who passed saw Majnoun in one of his usual spots, staring fixedly ahead, as he usually did. They did not see Hermes. The dogs, cats and birds, on the other hand, saw Hermes before they saw Majnoun and all were spooked.

There were a thousand questions Majnoun would have liked to ask. Are dogs greater than humans? Which beings are smartest? Why is there death? What is the purpose of life? Most of these questions were interesting, but their answers were now unimportant to Majnoun. Majnoun wished to know one thing and one thing alone: Nira's whereabouts. But he was afraid to ask the question or, rather, afraid of its answer. And Hermes – out of respect for Majnoun – did not speak of Nira. He waited, rather, to be asked.

Despite being unable to broach the one subject that mattered to him, Majnoun was more or less at ease in Hermes's company. They

146

spoke (silently) of a number of things, the god at home in the mind of the dog. And the day passed in what seemed moments.

As the sun set, Majnoun reluctantly left his station. He and Hermes wandered along Roncesvalles, drifting toward High Park. Majnoun sniffed at things on the ground, before Hermes led him to an alley behind a delicatessen. There, they found stale bread and a link of Polish sausage. Majnoun ate as much as he wanted, before wandering west to High Park. He was now well past the age of moving quickly and – in warm weather – he rarely went much farther than the park's perimeter: the playground, the duck pond, the trees near the streetcar roundabout.

When, at last, he and Hermes sat beneath the boughs of a pine tree, the question he'd avoided forced its way into his thoughts and Majnoun could not hide his anxiety.

– I can see, said Hermes, that you'd like to ask me something.

– Can you tell me what *love* means? asked Majnoun.

The sun had almost completely set. A crimson line lay just above the trees. The noises of night – subtler but more intriguing than those of day – had come, and the park was lit here and there by street light and moonlight. The shadows deepened.

– Your bodies are so graceful, said Hermes, and your senses are magnificent. I regret that you've been changed, Majnoun. If you were as you'd been, a dog like other dogs, the question you asked would not have occurred to you. You would know the answer already.

– The word reminds me of Nira, said Majnoun.

– I understand, said Hermes. So let us make a pact. I'll answer your question, but, in return, you'll consider leaving this place.

– I cannot leave without Nira, said Majnoun.

– I ask only that you consider it, said Hermes.

Majnoun agreed, then he sat up straight.

– What you want to know, Majnoun, is not what *love* means. It means no one thing and never will. What you want to know is what Nira meant when she used the word. This is more difficult, because Nira's word is like a long journey taken by one woman alone. She read the word in books, heard it in conversations, talked about it with friends and family, Miguel and you. No other being has encountered the word *love* as Nira has or used it in quite the same ways, but I can take you along Nira's path.

Which the god of translators did, taking Majnoun, in a handful of heartbeats, through every encounter Nira had had with the word *love*, allowing Majnoun to feel her emotions and know her thoughts each and every time she had heard, thought about or spoken the word: from the tiniest flicker of recognition to the deepest emotion and all points between. As Majnoun's understanding of Nira's 'love' deepened, so did his distress. Nira was restored to him as if she were there with them, but she was far from him as well, and it was suddenly unbearable to be without her.

Majnoun could not even keen, so overwhelmed was he by grief. All he could manage was a sigh. He lay down on the rust-coloured pine needles and put his head on the crux made by his paws.

– There's no need for you to wait any longer, said Hermes. I will take you to her.

At that moment, Majnoun would have done anything to see Nira again. And so, trusting in the god of thieves, he gave up his vigil. And his soul travelled through the evening with Hermes as its guide.

5

TWO GIFTS

Had there been a hint in Prince's poetry, a clear hint, that his was a soul on which a god might safely wager? No, not really. There was no clearly compelling reason to be optimistic about a dog that spent its time composing (and remembering) poems in a language unknown to all but a diminishing handful of dogs. In fact, by the time Prince composed his final poems, he was the only being on earth who could have understood them, the language of his pack having vanished almost as suddenly as it had come into being.

> Running through the grey-eyed dawn
> with last night's trash in mind,
> the brown dog scuttles
> through fluted gates
> while birds sing on above the world
> about a bit of fallen cheese,
> the shish kebob he ate
> and all the vagaries of plates
> that wait for him at home.

And yet, there *was* something. Prince's wit, his playfulness, was a curious element within him, a glittering depth. It was this, in the end, that the god of thieves had chosen to protect. Prince's spirit was a kind of quicksilver. The dog was as liable to die happy as it was to die miserable.

Prince was whelped in Ralston, Alberta, a mutt born to mutts born to mutts. It was impossible to say what breeds he had within him. He was medium-haired, russet-coloured with a white patch that covered his chest. There was almost certainly some golden retriever in him, and perhaps a touch of border collie. Not that his breeding mattered to the family that took him in. It certainly didn't matter to Kim, the youth who fed him, walked him, chased him across the prairie and hunted gophers with him.

Prince's character was partly innate, but it was also tempered by Kim, who encouraged his playfulness and his intelligence, and by Alberta itself, which, in its way, created him in its image. That is, the land allowed Prince to be a dog in a way that Albertan dogs are. For two years, Ralston was his home and his entire domain. He loved everything about it and about his life: from the way the prairie smelled in summer to the taste of his canned dog food, from the startling crack of a .22 rifle to the prospect of chasing down a wounded rodent, from the smell of Kim's bedroom to the affection he received from the entire family. In every way, the first two years of Prince's life were idyllic.

Then came exile. Kim moved from Ralston and took Prince with him. The journey itself was progressively distressing. They left on a cold morning in spring. It was early, but Prince imagined they were going to hunt rabbits and he was thrilled. The atmosphere was strange, though. It was unusually tense, and Prince could feel that Kim's mother was upset. Still, Kim's mother was often upset for no reason Prince could see, so he jumped into the car, excitedly sniffing at the air to get a whiff of rodent, ignoring the sound of her weeping and the peculiar stiffness of the family's demeanour.

Kim, in a shirt that smelled of soap and motor oil, left the window cracked open, so Prince, sneaking the tip of his nose out, could smell the dew-wet ground as the sun burned away the morning. How exhilarating it was! But then, familiar smells gave way to unrecognizable monotony: tar, dust, rock. The world began to look different. The beautiful distances of home become an increasingly oppressive closeness. And it began to seem as if they would never stop to hunt. Kim allowed him out of the car – on a leash – so he could pee in a small patch of lawn somewhere in the middle of a world that smelled of gasoline. They ate, eventually, and slept in the car before setting out again.

From there, the world grew more and more unknown: its sounds, its odours, the look of it as it flew by. All that Prince loved seemed to have vanished, leaving tall buildings, passing cars, an emptiness disguised as plenitude. They had reached the city.

Then, the city – which, in Prince's first days, was constantly bewildering – took Kim away from him as well. Perhaps, if Prince had had time to learn how to navigate the seemingly endless, linked mazes that made up the new world, he might have found Kim again. But he had not had time and, what's more, he could not understand how Kim could disappear. They had been wandering in a ravine through which a small river ran. There were trees and birds and, fatefully, squirrels. One moment, he and Kim were walking together, the next Prince was chasing a squirrel that ran up a side of the ravine.

The last he heard of Kim was

– Prince! Stay! Stay!

Kim was using his serious voice. In most circumstances, Prince would have returned to him at once. But the squirrel in question was insolent. It positively *wanted* biting. And then the trees and water, the smell of a world he thought he recognized: these things filled him with pleasure. Just running as he did, as fast as he could, was an exhilaration he was not certain he would ever feel again. It was all a wonderful game! So he'd run up the side of the ravine, where Kim couldn't easily follow, and then explored strange streets, going among houses that smelled of onions, paint and cooked flesh.

After a time, he stopped exploring. The game had finished. He began looking for Kim, but a door to one of the houses had opened and a woman had called him in and given him water and biscuits. How long he stayed at this house, he could not have said. He had barked to get out, but she had put him on a leash, taken him out for a walk, and kept him. Days or, perhaps, weeks later, he managed to get away. Naturally, he searched for Kim, but all trace of Kim was gone. Prince had wandered far from the ravine and he was lost in a bewildering maze of streets, bedevilled by sensations that were new and distracting.

The days that followed were grim. Even in Ralston – of which he'd known almost every inch by feel or smell – Prince could not be certain of human kindness. There'd been people around who'd chase him or throw stones. He'd gotten to know the worst of those and avoided them. But here, in this city, he did not know whom to avoid. So, he avoided all of them until hunger or thirst forced him to approach and beg.

Were it not that Prince had lost everything, you might say that he was, from here on, fortunate. After a week scrounging in the streets, overturning garbage cans, eating whatever he happened to find on the ground, he was taken in by a couple who treated him well. They fed him, gave him water, allowed him to stay in their home. He was disinclined to stay with them, whenever he remembered Kim, but at least they did not try to hurt him. They allowed him in or out of their house. So he returned to them.

They weren't entirely trustworthy, though. It was they who left him overnight in the clinic at King and Shaw.

The change affected Prince differently than it did any of the other dogs. Or it affected him more, in a rather specific way. Prince began to think about language, almost from the moment the change occurred. Names and naming seemed extraordinary to him and extraordinarily useful. It was an abstract idea, assigning a sound or a cluster of sounds to a thing. The concept wasn't foreign, of course. He associated the word *treat* with biscuits. In fact, this very association may have been at the root of his joy in language.

Whatever influenced his thinking about names and naming, however, he was not one to take anything too seriously. It was not his nature. He was the first creator of puns in the new language, as we've seen. But he was also the creator of one-liners and riddles. For instance

> – *How is a squirrel like a plastic duck?*
> – *They both squeak when you bite them.*

or, more metaphysically,

> – *Why do cats always smell like cats?*
> – *Oh look! A squirrel!*

To the casual listener, some aspects of Prince's jokes will, no doubt, be difficult to appreciate. To begin with, the first of anything is likely to be overwhelming, and these jokes, being the first in the pack's language, were not so much enjoyed as contemplated and admired. (By all the dogs.) The first one about the squirrel, for instance, seemed to be both true *and* fanciful, a correlation of things not usually correlated. Then there was the joke's linguistic mark: the word for 'squirrel' was extremely pleasurable to say. (All agreed about this as well.) Finally, there was Prince's performance. He needed to be heard in order to share the joy he took in language, but none of the other dogs were used to listening to the kinds of things Prince had to say. To hold their attention, Prince's demeanour, his diction and his delivery all had to be compelling. Although he'd had no previous experience as a raconteur, Prince invented a new manner of storytelling. It was for this that he was loved by those who loved him.

It was also for this new manner that he was hated. Not only did dogs like Atticus dislike Prince's perversions of their tongue, but neither could they deal with the implications of Prince. Here was a form of status – given through admiration for Prince's ability to speak and perform – that was so new it was difficult to think how one might combat it. What status was one to give to a dog whom one admired, but whose talents were so different than the traditional canine ones? What influence on the pack should the strange-speaking dog have? Was he dangerous? None of these questions was easily answered and so, in the end, it was fear that turned the conspirators against Prince.

His second exile – so strange and bewildering, coming as it did in the midst of a dream – was almost as devastating as the first. Prince could be forgiven for thinking that no world wanted him and, for some time, he suffered from what might be called depression. He wandered about the city finding ways to keep himself and his language – the language whose unofficial guardian he now was – alive. Yet, once again, despite his exile and bereavement, one could legitimately call Prince 'fortunate.' In the absence of home, of Kim and of his pack, there was at least one thing he loved, one thing that would be with him always: his pack's language.

As it happened, Prince's relationship to the language of his pack so influenced his outlook and personality that, as his time on earth drew to a close, Apollo grew increasingly uncertain about how the dog's life would end. This uncertainty affected him – god of plague and poetry – more than it did Hermes. Apollo was annoyed that a poet, of all things, might cost him his wager, but he also found it inconvenient not to know if he would win his younger brother's servitude. If there was one thing he disliked, it was losing to Hermes.

– Listen, he said to his brother, this creature has lived most of its life in exile. It's been unhappy for years. It can't have anything *but* an unhappy death. Why don't we settle our bet right now. If you like, I'll forget you doubled the penalty. Let's say you only owe me a year.

– No, said Hermes.

— You're sure? I mean, if I were you, I'd jump at the chance.

— If you're so sure, why don't we triple the bet? asked Hermes. Let's make it three years.

— You're not being serious, answered Apollo. You haven't been serious from the start. The premise was wrong on the face of it …

— Are you trying to reason with me? asked Hermes.

— There's no need to be insulting, said Apollo. I'm simply pointing out that you weren't being serious when you made this about the *moment* of death. If you asked a human to choose between a wonderful life with a terrible death or a miserable life with a wonderful death, which do you think it would choose? The *moment* of death is not important.

Hermes smirked.

— You *are* trying to reason with me, he said. In answer to your question: the young would choose an exciting life; the old a happy death. But none of that matters, since you agreed to the terms.

— You're right that it doesn't matter, said Apollo. This dog will die as miserably as the others, and I'll use you like a goat for a few years.

Apollo was upset, however. And as happens when the gods are angry, he took it out on a mortal. In this case, Prince. Though the dog was in the last months of its life, though Zeus had forbidden his sons from further interfering in the lives of the dogs, Apollo surreptitiously intervened in Prince's life. Making use of a handful of sand, he sent down afflictions to make the dog – now in its fifteenth year – suffer.

Over the years, Prince had explored much of the city, but he knew its middle and south best, preferring, in the end, the stretch of Toronto bounded by Woodbine, Kingston Road, Victoria Park and Lake Ontario. Dividing his time amongst a number of houses and masters, he had come to think of the Beach as home. He knew it intimately and loved some of its pleasures; for instance, going down from Kingston Road into the vegetal secret that was Glen Stewart Park. Then again there was the feel of the lakeshore in winter (the sand stiff) or the smell of it in summer: metal, fish, the oils that humans slathered on themselves.

Prince knew any number of safe paths through his territory: escape routes, shortcuts, diversions. He could – if he had to – sniff his way from Kingston near Main all the way to the bottom of Neville Park, from Kew Beach east and north to where Willow and Balsam meet. Certain streets he knew better than others, of course. Kingston Road, for instance. What a crooked loveliness! The way it meanders among the senses: strange spices, the humid entrances to Glen Stewart Park, fresh bread, unpredictable exhalations from houses, the staid and chemical smell of concrete buildings, the shimmer of streetlights and stoplights and all the illuminations of evening, the humans with their

– Tsk, tsk, tsk … here, boy!

a hand as it travels in the fur of your back as if searching for something, the sweetness of an unlikely perfume. Kingston Road was always familiar yet somehow always strange. Then again, what about Beech or Willow? They were among the avenues he did not know well. He recognized them by their smells and the way their names looked on street signs, but they were little more than ways to the lake, ways that shimmered in his memory: stretches of green and grey, lawns and sidewalk – dubious, hard to recall. But knowing a territory is knowing what is left to know. Beech and Willow were part of what Prince had left to explore, part of the Beach's great wealth.

Just as importantly, the Beach was where dogs were usually kept on leashes. This was a relief, because although, like Majnoun, Prince had learned to defend himself, he disliked having to subdue other dogs. For one thing, every dog dominated was one fewer to whom he could speak or teach his language. On occasion, he allowed himself to be bitten, but this was no better. Dogs who assumed they could dominate you made the poorest listeners. Then again, as he got older, it was more difficult to deal with those who were aggressive. So, odd though the thought was to him, Prince was grateful for leashes.

Then, too, the Beach was where humans, for the most part, left him alone. They had better things to do, it seemed, like keeping large balls in the air or gliding on shoes with small wheels or plunging themselves into the lake – whose waters reeked (marvellously) of urine, fish and a thousand dirty socks. The most serious problems Prince had with humans came when he was forced to defend himself against a dog that belonged to one of them. Humans could be brutal in defending their dogs and, what's more, Prince knew there would be difficulties if he bit one of them. So, on the rare occasions when humans attacked him, Prince ran for it, bolting over territory he knew as well as he had ever known territory.

Perhaps unsurprisingly, Prince's most moving poems were about the Beach. 'The Lake Comes to the Fringe,' for instance, was composed in 2011, during the summer before his death.

> The lake comes to the fringe
> while lights go up around the bay.
> Somewhere near, cow flesh is singed.
> Smoke floats above the walkway.
> I've eaten green that comes up black,
> risen cold from torrid mud.
> I've licked my paws and tasted blood.
> What is this world of busy lies?
> Some urban genie feeding food to flies!

With the Beach, in his final years, Prince had found a home again, at last. Cruel and unbiddable, Apollo took it from him.

To begin with, Prince lost his sight. Blindness descended on him over the space of two days, after a gust of wind sent sun-poisoned sand into his eyes and ears. At first, it was as if a grey mist hung over the world. The mist was thin but persistent: a softness, halos around sources of light, things in the distance vanishing as if behind an approaching white curtain. Then, the mist grew thick and close, as if it had turned to fog. Finally, all was grey and Prince could see nothing: no lights, no halos, no cars, no people, no buildings. Only a grey that was grey like grey blinkers over his eyes.

Though his blindness took time to efface the world, it was as traumatic as if it had come between one moment and the next. Prince was under the wooden staircase near the top of Glen Stewart Park when he realized that he could no longer see a thing. That is, he was well away from any of the homes that were 'his.' So, now blind, he had to make his way through the Beach to ... where, exactly?

Being an old but obviously bright dog, Prince was welcome in a handful of homes where he would be fed, petted and sheltered. The humans in these homes were all kind – none was as overbearing as Randy had been – but Prince had not wanted to be stuck in any particular house, choosing instead an independence that allowed him to explore his territory, to compose his poems in solitude, to encounter the world on his own terms. Also: after a few days, he inevitably grew tired of the behaviour his presence elicited in humans: cooing, fur rubbing, rolling about on the ground with him, smugness, condescension, chirpily rendered orders

– Here, boy! Here, boy!

– Roll over! Roll over!

and fluttering-voiced addresses

– Who's a good boy, eh? Who's a good dog?

No matter how much he tried to accept that their behaviour was dictated by their nature, Prince sometimes found human attention so distracting that he couldn't think straight. For this reason, in summer, he often stayed out, sleeping in whatever makeshift den he could find – bushes, benches, boxes, etc. In winter, it's true, he was forced to seek shelter, staying here or there for weeks at a time. But even in winter Prince tried to keep a certain distance from humans. Now that he was blind, with whom would he stay? Whose company would he choose, knowing that he might be with them for good?

There were only two homes he seriously considered. One belonged to a woman in a small house, far away from Glen Stewart and so far from the beach that he might not experience his beloved lake often enough. She was kind. She allowed him more freedom than any other human had, content to feed him and let him alone, patting him when she imagined he needed it. The woman smoked, however, the smell of cigarettes almost obliterating all others. And the 'feel' of her was sometimes frightening. From time to time, it was as if she longed to kill something. So the woman's place would not do as a permanent den. That left the house on Neville Park. It was on the edge of his territory, not far from the lake. The humans in it – a woman and three men – were all kindly disposed toward him. Even better: none clung to him or condescended. They put food down when he was there, let him out in the morning, let him back in the evening. The female paid the most attention to him, but he could bear her affection because she was not often demonstrative.

In general, humans were – as far as Prince was concerned – overly emotional and emotionally obvious. You could tell a human was angry from three blocks away, and that's without the creature growling, lunging or baring its teeth! They were beacons of emotion and it was often disruptive being near them. There were, of course, exceptions. Certain humans were unreadable or unstable. They could change mood in an instant, going from kindness to murderous intent without warning. He was very nearly kicked to death by one such, a man talking to himself on a park bench who called him over in a singsong voice and then kicked him hard in the ribs when he was in range. It was lucky for Prince that people had been around to protect him, but the incident confirmed his belief that humans were all – save Kim – potentially lethal. Naturally, this belief was at the back of his mind when he chose the house on Neville Park. The woman and three men had never been cruel to him, though there was always the chance they could turn.

Grey though the world was, it was still alive with scents: new scents, old scents, scents that were landmarks and others that, in their vivid-ness, threatened to lead him astray. The trees and the beams of the wooden steps and bridges gave off a familiar and comforting smell –

principally, dog's urine. As well, there were plant smells that he knew and could situate: this garden (at the edge of the park) with its flowers and weeds, that one with its vegetables. There was the smell of creek water, mud, dust, small animals, perfume, human sweat and bodies. He could, he felt, make his way to Queen Street, because his sense of smell was almost as acute now as it had been when he was younger. The real difficulty, he thought, would come not with the terrain itself but with the usual hazards: the humans in his way, dogs sniffing at him, and so on. But he fell down the first flight of steps he came to, smacking his head on the landing, his bearings momentarily lost.

How frightening it was to fall directionless into that grey nothing! Prince yelped instinctively. Once he'd recovered from the shock, however, he found that the pain was bearable – he'd known worse – and the fall taught him to be more cautious. Glen Stewart Park, familiar though it was, was hazardous. So he moved more deliberately, sniffing out every smell, listening for any danger, putting one paw cautiously in front of the next, trying to anticipate the flights of steps and the changes of direction the walkway took.

But he fell down the next flight of steps he came to as well. This time the pain was severe. It felt as if he had broken something inside. He yelped, then struggled to stand up. And when he was up on his legs, he was unsure of which direction he was facing, there being no up no down no to nor fro. The only good thing – if you could call it a good thing – was that he'd fallen off the wooden walkway and into the grass beside the spring that ran through the park. He would not have to worry about stairs, so long as he stayed beside the water. If he went in the right direction, he would find one of the roads out of Glen Stewart.

Despite his tendency to introspection, Prince was something of an optimist in hard times. Having a task to perform liberated him from himself. So it was that, now, having to make his way out of the park, he ignored his blindness – or, rather, accepted it – and went on his way as deliberately as he could, unsteady on his feet, his journey distracting him from worry. He made his way to Glen Manor Drive without too much trouble. He knew this stretch of ground (its smell and feel) so well that he scarcely had to think, his body doing the thinking (or remembering) for him. He found the path that rose up from the park to the road and then he followed the road down toward Queen, walking unsteadily on the sidewalk, looking like a drunken creature, until he came to the first corner.

Crossing a street was distressing in the best of circumstances. Glen Manor Drive was not busy – it was seldom busy – but cars always came at you so quickly. He had seen what they did to dogs who did not get out of the way. Their bodies were crushed into the road and left to rot until not even the hungriest things – blackbirds or maggots – would eat them. He preferred to cross at stoplights with humans around to shield him. Here, now, there were no lights and he was on his own and he could not help going slowly. He stood at the edge of the sidewalk for a long time, listening intently, and then, because he had to cross and knew it, he stepped onto the road, sniffing and listening, backing up suddenly on hearing a noise that *might* have been a car, almost losing his direction, before somehow making it to the distant point across the street, relieved to feel the step up to relative safety. And how wonderful to smell the great red house, its grounds, where he was sometimes fed and petted. He knew exactly where he was! He briefly considered begging at the house but he didn't want to risk being delayed there. So he went on.

The second corner was more difficult. He had to cross the street, then continue on around a curve where there was no sidewalk. He could see it in his mind. He knew where he was. He could smell Ivan Forrest Gardens before him to one side and the lake in the distance. He sat at the corner to collect himself, to ready himself for the crossing. It was then that he became conscious of humans approaching. No, what he heard was a group of humans bearing down on him: a crowd, it sounded like, coming fast, their soft-soled shoes slapping on the pavement, their breath escaping in collective gusts, and then the smell – sweat, rubber, genitals and dust. The wind brought it all to him like a foretaste of trouble.

What was going on? Was he in their way?

He made himself as unobtrusive as he could, curling his tail beneath him, crouching down. And then they were on him.

– Watch out for the dog!

Someone hit him.

– Christ on a cross! Get out of the way, doggy!

Someone hit him again, perhaps the same someone, stepping on his tail, pushing him aside. Prince yelped, made himself as compact as he could, then listened to the sound of them as they passed: feet slapping the road, dirt grinding on pavement, the soles of their shoes squeaking. Prince had always found these stampedes bewildering. But not knowing where the runners were coming from or how many there were made this instance alarming. At some point, one of the humans reached down to pat him on the head, and that contact, coming out of nowhere as it did, was the most frightening thing of all.

As suddenly as it was upon him, the stampede was gone, the sound of it receding. His heart beat violently and his body shook and it took him a long while – sitting at the intersection of Pine Crescent and Glen Manor – before he could go on without shaking. It occurred to him that it might be better to travel at night, to wait until all one could hear were crickets and the occasional, threatening shush of a passing car. But he pressed on, courageously stepping onto the street and making his way to the other side of Pine Crescent, then down into Ivan Forrest Gardens, where there were trails but no streets and no cars.

For a moment, as he made his way through Ivan Forrest, Prince almost forgot that he could not see. This was the part of his territory he knew best. He could navigate the terrain by the smell of his own urine alone. More: he could almost *see* the trees and posts where he had left his markings. He still went slowly, of course, the aches and pains of his body slowing him. He listened for humans, sniffed about for a piece of something to eat, stopped to accommodate such dogs as wanted to sniff his anus or genitals. Any fears he'd had that, vulnerable as he was, he might be attacked, were allayed. His fellow dogs could tell at once that he was in distress. They all expressed their sympathy, treating him with a kind of deference after licking his face and smelling his breath.

Prince spent what was left of the day in the gardens, recovering from a journey that would have taken him no time at all had he been younger or, even, sighted. That night, he slept close to a willow. He imagined himself hidden, but he was very nearly in the open, easily seen by all the creatures that walked, flew or crept past him on their way through the gardens.

In the early morning, he shivered himself awake and was almost surprised to discover that he was still blind. His blindness was so new it did not yet seem real. He was fifteen. His old bones – and his recent injuries from falling – made it painful for him to rise from the ground. His teeth chattered. The world was its morning self: quiet, the occasional, distant sound of a vehicle, the rattle and clang of the streetcar when it passed, the raw smell of a new day coming through the dew, mist and cold. He was disoriented and, now, more frightened than he'd been the previous day. He could smell the lake and he made his way toward it, leaving the park behind.

Prince had only one thing in mind: the house with the woman and three men. As it happened, circumstances favoured this part of his journey. There were few people about. Few people and few cars. He crossed Queen Street cautiously, stumbling like he was rabid, listening for cars or streetcars with every step. There were more streets to cross, more cars to listen for, but as he went south, the lake grew ever more present, leading him on to the end of the street where, all at once, the road was gone and he stumbled onto the boardwalk.

Even on his worst days, the lake buoyed his spirits. It was a measure of Prince's distress, on this morning, that he stopped only to take in the smell of it – licking his nose and moving it back and forth in the direction of the water – before carefully following the boardwalk, all the way to the bottom of Neville Park and up to what would be his last home.

Prince's first weeks in Neville Park were not unhappy, despite his blindness. He had survived a frightening journey, and the inspiration that came of survival – the exhilaration of having made it – carried him through the days, as he learned to negotiate the house without hurting himself.

He'd chosen his hosts well. The family took him in and they kept him even after discovering that he could no longer see. The woman in particular was kind. She put down food when it was time and took him for the short walks that were all he could manage, the aches and pains of his injuries in Glen Stewart almost crippling him, his deterioration quickening, it seemed, with his decision to settle in one place.

He missed his territory and his independence. In these first weeks, Prince would sometimes forget that he could not go out on his own until, forcing himself up to go to the door, he would bump into a chair or an appliance or a human. But there was compensation. As he accepted the idea that he would never see again, he began to rely on his memory and, in doing so, his memory became sharper (or, at least, more vivid), until he held a picture of the Beach in his imagination that he came to treasure almost as much as he had treasured the real thing.

Nor was death, whose approach he could feel, a source of worry. He thought about it, of course. He wondered when it would come and he mourned his ever-diminishing capacities, missing the things he had once taken for granted: sniffing out the breath of a dog he did not know, for instance, or running because the sheer pleasure of some great thing could not be expressed otherwise, or digging out bits of food half-buried in sand, or biting down on a newfound stick. The death that approached was a source of curiosity more than anything else. His final poems, which are among his most poignant, reflect Prince's mood.

'What is the name of he who comes' is the last poem he composed and it is characteristic of the work done while he was blind.

> What is the name of he who comes
> with eyes closed and fingers black,
> the one who draws the curtains back
> when dawn has come?
> 'Agha Thanatos' or just plain 'Death'?
> When will I know which is right?

Prince's poetry was, indirectly, the cause of his only true regret in the months before his death. As his strength faded, it became unavoidably clear that his work and his language would, with his death, disappear from the face of the earth. In the same way that the world had left him when he'd grown blind, so would his language leave the world. It would be effaced, all of the dogs who spoke it having died out.

To think that so necessary a thing could pass from the world so completely!

Was there nothing he could do to save it? Was there no way to pass it on? As he considered what might be done, Prince began to regret his attitude toward human language. He had avoided foreign languages, so that they would not influence his own. But had he learned another language, he might now have passed on his own. He had been selfish in trying to keep his language pure; better it had been influenced by another tongue than that it disappear altogether.

Though these thoughts brought him a real regret, Prince did not despair. He thought of what he had endured to reach the home he now had and he drew inspiration from what had been, in effect, a victory over blindness. It seemed to him that, frail though he was, it might not be too late, that he was perhaps fated to pass his work on to these people. That is why, in an heroic effort to preserve his language, Prince began to speak his poems to the woman. Whenever he could feel her presence or hear her voice, he would begin reciting.

— Grrr-ee arrr err oh uh ai
Gr-ee yurr ih aw yen grih yoo ayairrr …

No surprise: the woman took the sounds Prince made for the grumblings of an old and frail dog. She would pet him or hug him or scratch him behind the ears whenever he spoke. Prince found this distracting, but he persisted, reciting the same poem over and over, waiting for her to recite it back to him.

The more Prince did this, the more the woman tried to comfort him, because it did sound as if he were complaining about something. For one thing, like most poets, Prince's way of reciting his work was eccentric. He would sit up, trying to face the woman. Then, staying as still as he could, he would recite the first line, pause, then recite the second line, and so on. This in itself was strange for the woman. It would have been strange for any human who was not a poet.

— Are you okay, Elvis?

she'd ask, but as Prince had no idea what she was saying, he would simply carry on. He carried on until, eventually, it occurred to the woman that he was neither grumbling nor choking, but that he was *doing* something. In fact, after a week, she thought she recognized a pattern to his growls.

— Elvis isn't growling, she said to one of her sons. He's singing or something.

Her son, however, would have none of it.

— Mom, he's old and his mind's going, that's all.

— I suppose you're right, she said.

But she was not convinced and, one day, as a kind of lark, she repeated Prince's grumblings back at him. Prince immediately stopped and barked happily. He repeated the passage she had repeated to him. And again, the woman spoke (poorly and with a strange accent, but still …) a few lines of his verse.

— Grrr-ee arrr err oh uh ai
Gr-ee yurr ih aw yen grih yoo ayairrr …

Here was a real breakthrough. Prince was profoundly grateful. It seemed to him that a great boundary had been crossed. But Apollo, ever implacable, was not finished with him. The woman's version of his verse was the last thing Prince heard on earth. He then became stone deaf. He could not even hear himself, feeling only the vibrations his body produced when he tried to make a sound. This was a devastation. The world and all his versions of the world were taken away from him at once.

Prince was not one to lose hope, but now hope abandoned him. He was alone in endless grey silence, his sense of smell and balance the only acute senses left to him. Now and then, he would be picked up by one of the men and put somewhere. This was the most disconcerting thing of all. Without warning, he would be at someone's mercy, in someone's arms. It helped that he could recognize the men by their smell, but it did not help much. Tired, old, deaf and blind, Prince knew his time had come and he tried to meet his fate with as much dignity as he could muster.

He stopped eating and drank little. He retreated into the depths of himself and waited for a death that did not take long. One morning, he was picked up by the woman. He could feel her emotion. They were going somewhere, but Prince was too weak to mind. Outside, he felt the air on his muzzle. The lake came to him, its presence like a long-forgotten dream. It was a consolation. Then they were travelling in a car, a sensation that reminded him of Kim, and that too was consoling. And Prince allowed himself to be consoled, his mood little influenced by the smells of the veterinary clinic, though he knew this – the smell of soap, chemicals, other animals – was almost certainly the end.

One would have said, just before Prince died, that Apollo had won his bet, that none of the dogs had died happy, that they had died as miserably or more so than humans did. Lying quietly on a metal table, too tired to object, Prince was despondent about the loss of his language. But then, as those around him went about the business of killing, one of his last poems returned to him. He heard it in his mind as if someone were reciting it, almost as if it were not his at all. At that exact moment it struck him again how beautiful his language was. Certainly, if he was the last of his pack, it was sad that no creature alive knew it. But how wonderful that he – unexceptional though he had been – had been allowed to know it as deeply as he had. He had not explored all of its depths, but he had seen them. And so it occurred to Prince that he had been given a great gift. More: it was a gift that could not be destroyed. Somewhere, within some other being, his beautiful language existed as a possibility, perhaps as a seed. It would flower again. He was certain of it and the certainty was wonderful.

And so, against all expectations, Prince's spirits soared.

In a word, he was happy as death came for him at last.

As Prince lay dying, Apollo and Hermes were once again at the Wheat Sheaf Tavern.

Speaking of the dog, Apollo said

– All right. I concede. The creature dies happy. It's all been very instructive.

– No, no, said Hermes. Two years of servitude, *that* will be instructive.

– You do remember that you owed me ten, don't you? This just brings it down a little.

– My luck's changed, said Hermes. I can feel it.

– You're right about it being luck, said Apollo.

And he protested, theatrically, that the wager had been unfair. His protests were not serious, however. Yes, it annoyed him that he had been cruel to one of his own, that a poet should be the reason for this loss to his brother, but, really, it was a matter of pure chance who died happy and who did not. Which is why, of course, he and Hermes had bet on the outcome in the first place.

The bartender, a devout young woman, approached, her head bowed, unable to look at the gods directly.

– Is there anything I can get for you? she asked. Anything at all? I would be honoured.

– I like this Labatt's, said Apollo. Give me another.

— You like it? said Hermes. It's a waste of perfectly good water.

— Philistine! said Apollo.

The brothers laughed. The bartender went off to get a Blue.

— It would have been different if we'd given cats this so-called intelligence, said Apollo.

— It would have been exactly the same, said Hermes. What we should have done was give a human the intelligence and capacities of a dog.

— I'm tired of this business, answered Apollo. Let's talk about something else.

For a moment, they talked about Olympian matters, but then Apollo said

— I wonder what would happen if we gave one of these creatures our language?

— Our language? said Hermes. No mortal could learn so many shades of silence.

— I didn't say teach, said Apollo. I said *give*.

— You've been down here too long, answered Hermes. Let's go home. Hephaestus owes me some of his winnings.

— You go, said Apollo. I'll stay a little longer.

The sky was a light red as Hermes left the Wheat Sheaf. A car stopped, blasting music so loud that its chassis shivered as it idled at the corner of King and Bathurst, waiting for the lights to change. Inside, the driver was immobile, save for the index finger of his right hand, which tapped the steering wheel in time to the beat.

What was there to say about these creatures, really? He knew almost infinitely more than did the man at the wheel. He knew more about him than the man knew about himself. He knew more about every human, insect and animal the man would ever come in contact with. Beyond knowledge, he also possessed power no mortal could fathom. Had he wished, he could have crushed the car, or the city block on which it stood. Had he wished, he could have broken one of the man's fingers or torn a single hair from one of his eyebrows.

He could have granted the man everything he wanted or taken everything from him. For all the creature's 'humanity' or 'dignity' or whatever it was they congratulated themselves on possessing, the man in the car was an almost insignificant aspect of the god's being.

And yet, a divide existed between them, one that the god could not breach, despite his power, knowledge and subtlety: death. On one side, the immortals. On the other, these beings. He could no more understand what it was to live with death than they could what it was to exist without it. It was this difference that fascinated him and kept him coming back to earth. It was at the heart of the gods' secret love for mortals. Death was in every fibre of these creatures. It was hidden in their languages and at the root of their civilizations. You could hear it in the sounds they made and see it in the way they moved. It darkened their pleasures and lightened their despair. Being one of those who longed for death, Hermes found the earth and all its mortals fascinating, perhaps even at times worthy of the depths he allowed himself to feel for them. It is this, of course, this 'feeling' whose nature surpasses language or human understanding, that kept Hermes – that kept *all* the gods – from wiping mortals out.

On the one hand, power; on the other, love.

The light changed. The car drove off, and Hermes, imperceptible, rose above the city. To the south, the lake was a light mauve. The clouds above the water were airy and white. Hermes's thoughts turned to Prince. How odd that such a perceptive creature had imag-ined the death of a language would mean the death of its poetry. For the immortals, all true poetry existed in an eternal present, eternally new, its language undying. Having once been uttered, Prince's verse would live forever. At the thought of the dog, Hermes was pleased. And, feeling magnanimous, the god of translators rewarded Prince for his artistry and his unwitting service.

Prince's soul, which had almost entirely extricated itself from the world, returned briefly to consciousness. He was in a stretch of green and ochre prairie that smelled of Ralston. He was young again, and how thrilling it was to have his senses alert and vivid. It was a late afternoon in summer, somewhere around four o'clock. The sun had just begun to cede its ground to darkness. In the distance were the yards behind the houses on Cawnpore Crescent. He could smell the spore of a gopher, urine, pine gum, dust and the burning flesh of lamb that wafted toward him from god knows where.

Suddenly, he heard a voice that he loved.

– Here, Prince! Here, boy!

It was Kim, the only human whose name he had ever bothered to keep. Prince could see him in the distance, Kim's silhouette unmistakable for any other. And Prince's soul was filled with joy. He ran to Kim as he always did: with abandon, bounding over the prairie. This time, though, he ran having caught every nuance in Kim's voice, understanding him fully.

In his final moment on earth, Prince loved and knew that he was loved in return.

Toronto, 2013
Quincunx 2

A NOTE ON THE TEXT

The poems in *Fifteen Dogs* are written in a genre invented by François Caradec for the OULIPO. It was invented after François Le Lionnais, a founder of the group, wondered if it were possible to write poetry that has meaning for both humans and animals. In *Fifteen Dogs*, each poem is what Caradec called a 'Poem for a dog.' That is, in each poem the name of a dog will be audible – to the listener or to the dog – if the poem is said aloud, though the name is not legible. Here is an example by Harry Mathews. It is a poem written for Elizabeth Barrett Browning's dog, Flush:

> My Mistress never slights me
> When taking outdoor tea
> She brings sweet cake
> For her sweet sake
> Rough, luscious bones for me.

In Mathews's poem, between the words *rough* and *luscious*, the name *Flush* can be heard. In the same way, each of the poems in Fifteen Dogs contains one of the dogs' names.

The poem containing the name 'Prince' was written by Kim Maltman.

As well, Kim collaborated on the writing of two other poems ('Ronaldinho' and 'Lydia') and edited all fifteen 'poems for a dog.'

The song Majnoun hears beside High Park (p. 123) is based on lines written by Roo Borson.

Prince's metaphysical 'riddle' was suggested by Alex Pugsley.

Typeset in Albertan and Gotham.

Albertan was designed by the late Jim Rimmer of New Westminster, B.C., in 1982. He drew and cut the type in metal at the 16pt size in roman only; it was intended for use only at his Pie Tree Press. He drew the italic in 1985, designing it with a narrow fit and a very slight incline, and created a digital version. The family was completed in 2005, when Rimmer redrew the bold weight and called it Albertan Black. The letterforms of this type family have an old-style character, with Rimmer's own calligraphic hand in evidence, especially in the italic.

Printed at the old Coach House on bpNichol Lane in Toronto, Ontario, on Zephyr Antique Laid paper, which was manufactured, acid-free, in Saint-Jérôme, Quebec, from second-growth forests. This book was printed with vegetable-based ink on a 1965 Heidelberg KORD offset litho press. Its pages were folded on a Baumfolder, gathered by hand, bound on a Sulby Auto-Minabinda and trimmed on a Polar single-knife cutter.

Edited and designed by Alana Wilcox
Cover design by Ingrid Paulson
Maps on pp. 10–11 by Evan Munday

Coach House Books
80 bpNichol Lane
Toronto ON M5S 3J4
Canada

416 979 2217
800 367 6360

mail@chbooks.com
www.chbooks.com